Kang Youwei's Overseas Poetry Collection

(Chinese/English)

康有为海外诗集

中英双语版

康有为／著 〔加〕张启礽／注 〔美〕康雪培／译

Written by Kang Youwei Annotated by Zhang Qireng Translated by Kang Xuepei

青岛市城市文化遗产保护中心 编

Compiled by Qingdao City Cultural Heritage Protection Center

中国出版集团

中译出版社

图书在版编目（CIP）数据

康有为海外诗集 : 汉文、英文 / 康有为著 ; (加) 张启礽注 ; (美) 康雪培译. -- 北京 : 中译出版社, 2025. 1. -- ISBN 978-7-5001-8102-6

Ⅰ. I222.749

中国国家版本馆CIP数据核字第2024N8A388号

康有为海外诗集（中英双语版）

KANG YOUWEI HAIWAI SHIJI: ZHONG-YING SHUANGYU BAN

出版发行： 中译出版社
地　　址： 北京市西城区新街口外大街28号普天德胜大厦主楼 4 层
电　　话：（010）68359827；68359303（发行部）；68359725（编辑部）
传　　真：（010）68357870　　**电子邮箱：** book@ctph.com.cn
邮　　编： 100088　　**网　　址：** http://www.ctph.com.cn

出 版 人： 刘永淳　　**出版统筹：** 杨光捷
总 策 划： 范　伟　　**策划编辑：** 刘瑞莲　范祥镇
责任编辑： 刘瑞莲　　**执行编辑：** 杨佳特
营销编辑： 吴雪峰　董思嫄
封面设计： 潘　峰

排　　版： 北京中文天地文化艺术有限公司
印　　刷： 中煤（北京）印务有限公司
经　　销： 新华书店

规　　格： 880 毫米 × 1230 毫米　1/32
字　　数： 160千字　　**版　　次：** 2025年1月第1版
印　　张： 10.375　　**印　　次：** 2025年1月第1次

ISBN 978-7-5001-8102-6　　**定价：** 68.00元

康有为在槟榔屿，1903 年

皇清誥封宜人
晋封一品夫人
顯妣
勞太夫人像
賜進士出身誥授光祿大夫
頭品頂戴弼德院副院長男康有爲題

康有为的母亲劳太夫人

上：康有为父女访问阿伯丁女子小学，1904 年 10 月

下：何氏家庭合影（后站立者为康有为三夫人何旃理），1907 年，于美国斐士那

左：康同璧丈夫罗昌牛津大学毕业照，1905 年

右：康有为二夫人梁随觉及其所生子女

康有为七十大寿留影，于上海延香堂

康有为最后两首文岛诗的手稿

康有为次女康同璧 1903 年留影于温哥华，此照片出自《康同璧南温莎旧藏》
她陪同父亲游历各国，并担任翻译

Kang Tongbi, the second daughter of Kang Youwei, accompanied her father to travel during her vacations, serving as his interpreter

目录 Table of Contents

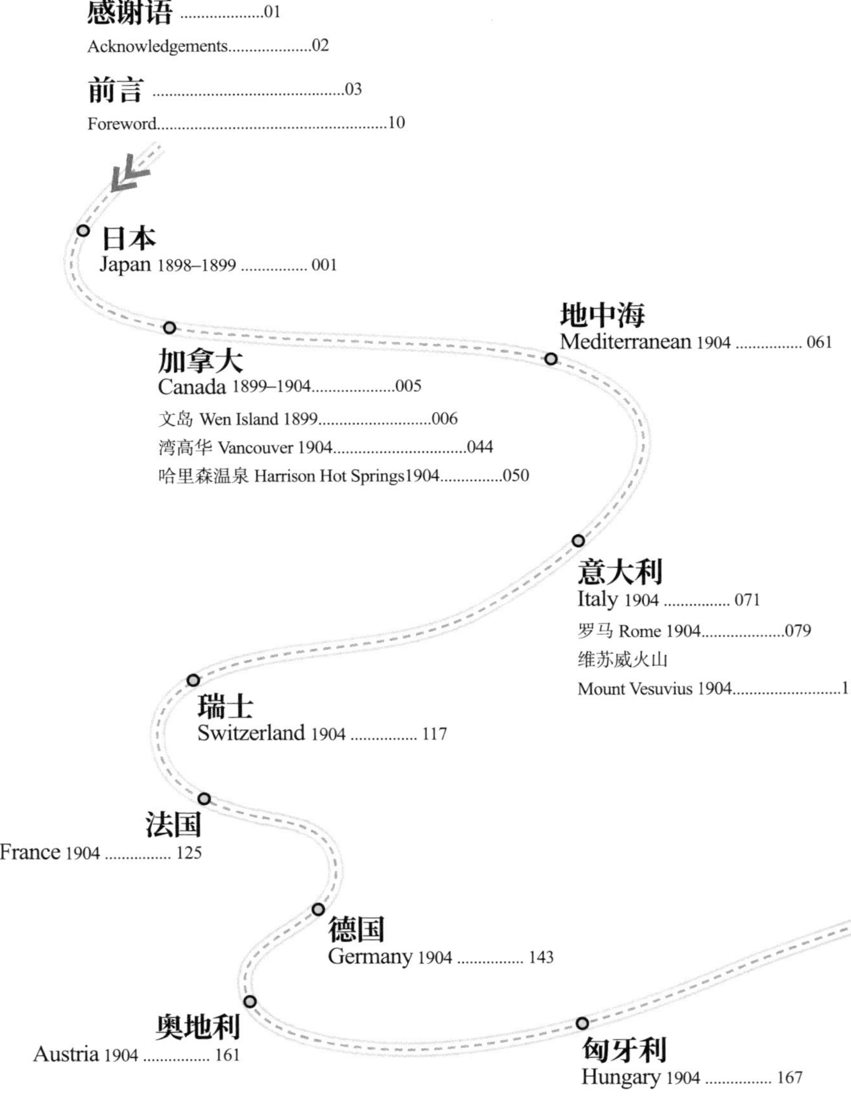

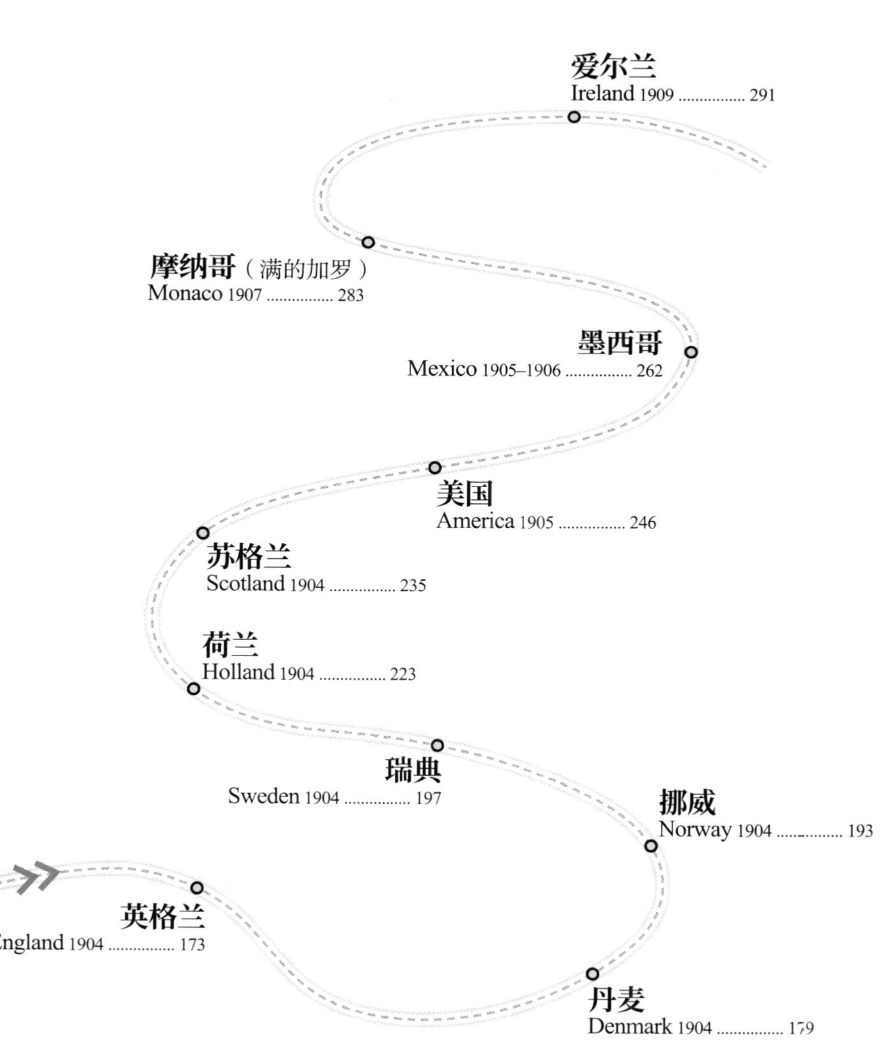

感谢语

《康有为海外诗集》(中英双语版) 的成功出版，离不开美国朋友约翰·Z 先生的大力支持和热情帮助。约翰·Z 先生花大量时间认真仔细地检查我们翻译成英文的诗和注文，并提供了及时的专业的编辑帮助，以及提出有建设性的意见。正是在他的帮助下，我们才能一步步前进，最后抵达终点站——完成了这本《康有为海外诗集》(中英双语版)。

接下来，我们要特别感谢好朋友王庆苏女士，她对我们这个翻译项目给予了大力的支持。正是因为有她不断的关心和鼓励，我们才把这个尝试翻译几首诗后就停下来的项目，重新拾起并继续下去。也正是通过庆苏，我们认识了她的丈夫约翰·Z 先生，并且请他担任我们的英语编辑。作为一名双语精通者，庆苏时常在一旁解释难解之处，为约翰编辑的精准度提供了非常及时且有价值的帮助。

衷心地感谢广东佛山市南海区丹灶镇人民政府和青岛市城市文化遗产保护中心在我们编译、编辑和出版的过程中所给予的热情鼓励和大力支持。

康雪培 (休斯敦)

张启礽 (温哥华)

2023 年 9 月

Acknowledgements

Completing this anthology of *Kang Youwei's Overseas Poetry Collection* in both Chinese and English would have been almost impossible without the help we received from several people. First of all, we owe a special measure of gratitude to Mr. John Z for his taking time to go through all the poems translated into English and providing prompt, insightful and professional editorial help and useful suggestions and comments. It was with his help, we were able to move forward one step at a time till we finally completed this anthology.

Next, we owe a special measure of gratitude to Qingsu Wang, my dear friend, for her interest in our translation project. It was from her cheering and encouraging words that we picked up the stopped-in-the-middle project and continued it to completion. It was also through Qingsu that we got to know her husband Mr. John Z who then became our most helpful editor. As a bilingual, Qingsu's useful suggestions and comments were timely and valuable.

Finally, our profound thanks go to the Danzao Town Government, Nanhai District, Foshan, Guangdong, and Qingdao Heritage Cultural Protection Center for their great encouragement and support in bringing this book to fruition.

Kang Xuepei, Houston, Texas
Chang Chi Jeng, Vancouver, British Columbia
September 2023

前 言

1898年的中国清朝，实行了仅一百零三天的维新变法（又称戊戌变法），因保守统治势力慈禧太后突发政变而失败。光绪皇帝被软禁，包括康有为胞弟康广仁在内的六位维新领袖被处决。慈禧下令残酷镇压变法，并以十万美金的高价，悬赏抓捕变法领袖康有为。在英国和日本政府的帮助下，康有为成功地逃出国，从此流离失所，浪迹天涯。

从1898年到1913年，在逃亡海外的十六年间，康有为行程六十万里，游遍四洲三十一国。基于康有为本身强烈的全球意识和开放精神，他的被迫流亡使得他向西方寻找真理的强烈愿望得以实现，使他成为中国有史以来出游时间最长、行经地域最广、收获最大的旅行家。1904年12月，他在加拿大文岛完成了《欧洲十一国游记》序，并于1905年出版《欧洲十一国游记第一编·意大利游记》和《欧洲十一国游记第二编·法兰西游记》，都是他流亡时期的主要著作。

当今国内对康有为的研究呈现出一种倾向，即较普遍关注康有为的早期生平及其维新改革思想，而对康有为流亡海外多年的政治思想、所作所为和生活少有触及，形成了康有为研究状况趋于重前期轻后期、重国内轻海外的现象。这与百年前的落后通信不无关系。学术界有些片面不当的说法：康有为的黄金期是在前期而不在后期。这个说法影响了对康有为人生的全面解析和研究，导致了康有为研究链条环节中出现薄弱处和缺失。

康有为流亡海外是在他生命中精力最旺盛的壮年期间。漫长的十六年岁月是不能简单数笔带过的。事实上，康有为的海外流亡岁月已被证明是他一生中最活跃、经历最丰富、最富有成就的时期。康有为是位坚定的爱国者，虽然远离了祖国，但他仍用实际行动证明了自己一生报效祖国的热忱心志。康有为于1898年10月24日由香港到达日本后，做的第一件事就是试图说服日本政府，要求其出面，向慈禧为首的清政府交涉光绪皇帝的囚禁事件。日本政府碍于自身利益未做反应。康有为便于1899年4月3日到达加拿大，之后多次试图从加拿大进入美国，但都被美国拒绝入境。在加拿大期间，康有为作为光绪皇帝的雄辩代言人，呼吁广大华人团结起来，为被囚禁的皇上和危机四伏的祖国抗议发声。他十次濒死逃亡的经历也深受华侨的同情。加拿大华侨的爱国热情就这样被熊熊点燃起来。

当时康有为仍将希望寄托于英政府，指望英国伸出援手对慈禧太后施压，还皇权于光绪皇帝。他于5月20日离开加拿大赴伦敦，5月31日抵达。英国为康有为的请求召开议会，但由于保守势力强，先进的革命党派只占少数，请求没有通过。无奈之下，康有为重返加拿大。多次的失败使康有为认识到求助他国是无济于事的，他决定自己立即行动，团结组织加拿大华人爱国人士，并于7月19日在当地成立了“保救大清皇帝会”，即保皇会。保皇会是一个过渡性政党，顾名思义就是要保护皇帝，并寻找途径来拯救祖国，继续推进维新改革事业。继温哥华和维多利亚二埠的保皇会成立后，各地华人闻风而动，纷纷建立保皇分会。在短短的三个月里，就有三十几个分会相继成立。康有为致信世界各地华人“创保皇会以救圣主，而救中国”，呼吁华人为自己的祖国安危成立保皇会。就这样，保皇会迅速发展成了声势浩大的全球性华人组织。保皇会存在的十余年间，其分会发展到北美、南美、亚洲、非洲和大洋洲五大洲，先后建立了约三百个分会，成为当时世界上最大的华人组织。

保皇会同志会牌
The Copper Badge for Comrades of Chinese Reform and Association

康有为身在海外，心系祖国。他日夜挂念在囚禁中的皇上，也为了他人生的终极目标——在中国实行君主宪政制的改革费心费神。在海外的生活环境里，他担任起多重新的角色：政治家、华侨领袖、商人和旅游家。他所到之处，成立华文学校，以弘扬中华文化，培养爱国情操；开设中国银行，创办中文报纸，以流亡者的身份与各国总统、国王和总理会面，切磋政治和社会问题。他还带领海外华

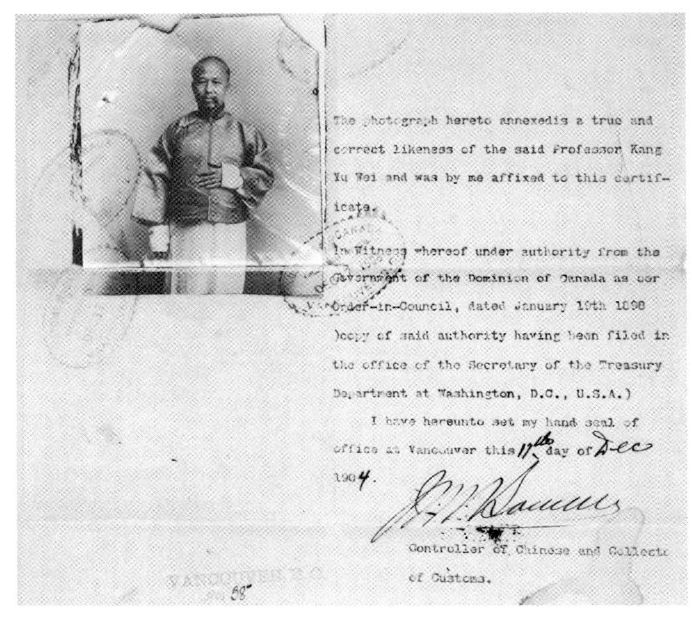

The photograph hereto annexedis a true and correct likeness of the said Professor Kang Yu Wei and was by me affixed to this certificate.

In Witness whereof under authority from the Government of the Dominion of Canada as per Order-in-Council, dated January 19th 1898)copy of said authority having been filed in the office of the Secretary of the Treasury Department at Washington, D.C., U.S.A.)

I have hereunto set my hand seal of office at Vancouver this 17th day of Dec 1904.

Controller of Chinese and Collecto
of Customs.

VANCOUVER B.C.

加拿大颁发给康有为的旅游证书
照片来源：青岛康有为故居纪念馆
Picture source: Qingdao Kang Youwei Former Residence Museum
C.I.6 Certificate Dec.1904

人共同反对种族歧视，争取在居住国里获得平等的人权和待遇。

康有为的流亡者身份使他能够涉足深广。首先，基于他执着的政治倾向和时间上的紧迫感，他把旅行的主要目的放在考察欧洲国家的政府模式、政治制度、风土文化等上面。其次，他把兴趣也放在了参观当地的文物古迹上，包括博物馆、画廊、宫殿、精英故居等。

年轻时的康有为不满足于老师灌输给他的儒家传统式

的为社会服务的理念。他的叛逆心理和好奇心驱使他将兴趣转向西方社会。他如饥似渴地阅读西方政治、历史和文化领域的译文书籍。大量有关欧洲社会政治和历史的阅读使他对西方文明产生了敬佩之情。他年轻的心完全向外面的世界敞开了。1880年代，他就开始构思起乌托邦“大同社会”的基本思想——历史进步、社会平等、世界政府和宇宙本质的思想。欧洲一些国家的历史和发展模式曾被他作为中国改革的典范。他坚定的政治思想走向和强烈的社会改革精神在他的游记和诗歌中处处可见。

在旅途中，康有为热衷于了解外国社会时事，目的是将来可把外国的历史发展和运作实例用作祖国强国建设的标准和榜样。无论走到哪里，康有为都会用心写下详细的游记，其中很大一部分以他惯用的诗歌形式表达。本书收录的康有为游记诗，仅是他865首游记诗总数中的冰山一角，是表达他思想、兴趣的、诗歌和游记的代表作。

康有为的旅行诗作以叙事抒怀居多，是他观古物、雕塑、博物馆等触景生情后的有感而发。联想中国近代历史上的不幸和社会现状，他深深地为国家兴亡担忧。观景生情，思乡思国，心潮起伏，指陈中外，是维新诗人救国无门的悲情感怀和慨叹，也是诗人抒怀诗情景交融的最大亮点。欧洲各国的奇丽风景令诗人大感赏景之趣，细腻生动的描述出自诗人的观景细致、思维广阔，以奇句写奇景，令读者身临其境、同感同悟是诗人风景诗魅力的所在之处。

康有为游记诗的一个显著特点是大量的隐喻用典。诗人从小博览群书，中国古代文学的扎实功底和对古体诗的熟练掌握，使其对相宜的古代典故可以信手拈来，轻松集句成联，巧妙借古喻今，浑然天成地写出了一首首磅礴大气、凝练沉郁的诗歌。诗人在欧洲历史、文化、风土人情方面的广博知识，也使他能够巧用欧洲“异国情调”的历史典故来反映中西方文化的接触和碰撞。诗人以历史学家的视角，通过对欧洲战后社会、政治、文化的密切观察，围绕自己的改革思想和祖国强盛的最终目标，用诗的形式发表自己的思考和评论，是康有为游记诗的独特风格。

必须承认的是，康有为诗作中频繁运用的中国古代典故和欧洲历史背景的隐喻，会使当今大多数读者有望而却步的感觉。因此，康有为诗作的读者和其诗歌的评论研究都相对有限。针对这种情况，此诗集设为中英双语版，旨在向中国读者普及康有为的海外游记诗，以及为那些对中国近代改革家康有为旅游诗感兴趣的西方读者开拓一个途径。任何具有基础英语知识的人都可以通过英语翻译这个桥梁，轻松阅读欣赏。游记诗里大量寓意隐晦的古代典故，经过翻译成通俗易懂的英文，让人有一种豁然顿悟之感，这无疑会成为学习中国文学典故的一个很好的读物。而令人费解的古老欧洲历史典故经翻译转化为日常英语后，成为妙趣横生的历史故事，是学习欧洲历史的有趣方式。本书的翻译着重于维护历史的真实性，传达诗人的意境和内心世界，从语言、风格、结构、语法全然不同的古文汉语转换成流畅的英语，同时要创造英语诗歌的韵律和诗意，让诗歌阅读成为一种享受和学习兼得的美好体验。

康有为十六年的海外岁月，可以用“旅行”二字来高度概括，也是他旅行生涯的精简描述，正如本书封面上康有为本人最喜欢用的旅行印章上的文字：“维新百日，出亡十六年，三周大地，游遍四洲，经三十一国，行六十万里。”康有为是天生的诗人，他独特的风格和诗韵，不失为中国诗坛上令人刮目相看的诗作。他的无数次旅行，从某种意义上可以说是文化之旅、历史之旅、心灵之旅。这些旅行经历以其卓越的诗歌创作力被写成游记诗，也不失为研究中国近代史，和近代史上绕不过的改革大家康有为的上好的文化素材。

康有为，1905 年摄于美国
Kang Youwei in U.S.A, 1905

Foreword

“悬赏十万美金的高价捉捕变法领袖康有为”
A Woman Would Give $100,000 for the Head of this Chinaman

In 1898, the Hundred Days Reform (also: WuXu Reform戊戌变法) in China, which lasted only 103 days, failed due to a sudden coup d'état engineered by the conservative ruling force Empress Dowager Cixi. The emperor Guangxu was placed in confinement, six of the reform leaders, including Kang's own brother, were executed. Empress Dowager Cixi ordered a cruel suppression of the reform movement and offered a high reward of 100,000 dollars for the head of the principal leader of the reform movement, Kang Youwei. With the help of the British and Japanese governments, Kang Youwei successfully escaped abroad, and became a homeless exile for about 16 years.

From 1898 to 1913, Kang Youwei traveled 600,000 *li* [1] (about 186,000 miles) and visited thirty-one countries on

1 *Li*, mileage in Chinese, equals to ½ kilometer.

four continents during his sixteen years of exile overseas. Owing to Kang Youwei's strong global consciousness and open spirit, his forced exile became an important opportunity for him to seek truth from the West and made him an unprecedented traveler who traveled the longest in terms of time, most in terms of places, and highest in terms of accomplishment throughout the history of China. In December 1904, he completed the preface to *Travel Notes of Eleven Countries in Europe* on Wen Island, Canada, and published *Travel Notes of Italy* and *Travel Notes of France,* both of which were the main works during his exile period.

Today, there has been a tendency in China, in the study and research of Kang Youwei, to generally focus on the early stage of Kang's life and his reform ideology rather than the later stage of his life overseas, with an emphasis on his political thinking during the era of transition. It is understandable that the travel accounts Kang had written overseas were hardly available in China due to inefficient communication a century ago. Therefore, the assertion that Kang Youwei's golden age was in his early stage of life rather than his later stage is quite one-sided and inappropriate. Such a misleading assertion has caused a weak or a missing link in the chain of the study and research of Kang Youwei's whole life.

Sixteen years in Kang Youwei's prime time of life is by no means short and should not be neglected. In fact, Kang's life in exile has been proven as his most active and productive period of his life. Being away from his home country, Kang Youwei, a steadfast patriot, proved himself a man of action. After he first successfully escaped from Hong Kong to Japan on October 24, 1898, he tried to persuade the Japanese and British governments to intervene for the emperor's safety and freedom. Obtaining no help, Kang Youwei went to Canada on April 3, 1899 in an attempt to enter America afterwards via Canada, yet he was unable to get a visa. He stayed in Vancouver. Acting as an eloquent spokesman on behalf of the Emperor, Kang gave many speeches to the Chinese living in Vancouver. His calling for saving the Emperor Guangxu in confinement, and saving the home country in turmoil, as well as his own ten near-death experiences escaping from the soldiers of Cixi regime won deep sympathy and active support from the listeners, igniting their patriotic enthusiasm to a high pitch.

On May 20, 1899, Kang Youwei started on a special trip to London in a second effort to plead for British government's support. He arrived in London on May 31. Once again, his pleading was unsuccessful. Having realized there was no use relying on foreign forces to save China, Kang Youwei went back to Canada and wasted no time in uniting Chinese patriots in Canada. He established the Chinese Baohuanghui (保皇会), a transitional political party popularly known as "Chinese Empire Reform Association" in July that year. The primary goal was to bring Emperor Guangxu back into power and find some way to carry out the reform, thereby saving the country. Then he was able to enter America after he got a visa. There he traveled to various places, all the while working on organizing the Chinese immigrants around his patriotic projects to save China. Adding to the two Chapters of Baohuanghui in Vancouver and Victoria, about ten more Chapters along the west coast of America were quickly established. Kang Youwei then issued an open letter to the Chinese throughout the world to promote the establishment of Baohuanghui Chapters for their home country China. The open letter was well received and garnered many positive responses. Baohuanghui developed into a global organization within a few years, its over two hundred chapters covering five continents: North America, South America, Asia, Africa and Australia.

Being in exile overseas, there never was a single day that Kang Youwei didn't think of his Emperor in confinement and his goal of Monarchist reform in China. He presented himself in a multitude of new persona: as politician, statesman, businessman, the leader of the overseas Chinese and most of all, a chronic traveler who established quite a few Chinese schools at different places to promote Chinese culture and cultivate patriotic sentiments, opened Chinese banks, found Chinese Newspapers, and met with presidents, kings, and prime ministers from various countries. He also led the overseas Chinese to fight actively against racial discrimination and strive for equal rights and treatment in the country they lived in.

Kang Youwei's status as a homeless exile allowed him to travel extensively. Guided by his strong political obsession and pushed by a sense of emergency, Kang set his primary traveling purpose as the investigating, with an emphasis on government models, political institutions, and local customs of European countries. Secondly, he put in his interests in visiting cultural relics and historic sites, including museums, galleries, palaces, and elites' former residences, etc. Traveling with a defined purpose, he was constantly on the move.

When Kang Youwei was young, his inquisitive and rebellious mind made him unsatisfied with the conventional Confucian ideal of service to society that his teachers instilled in him. He turned his interest to western societies and read voraciously translations of western books in the realms of history, politics and culture. As a result, he acquired a large amount of knowledge about European social politics and history and came to admire Western civilization. His young mind was fully opened up by the outside world. In the 1880s, he began to conceive some of his basic Utopian ideas: ideas of historical progress, social equality, one world government, and the nature of the universe. The history and development models of some European countries were used by him as models for the reform in China. His key-concept of ideological foundation and strong sentiment of reform were evident throughout his travel accounts and poems.

While traveling, Kang Youwei was always an attentive enthusiast of current affairs in foreign societies, keen on taking examples of historical development and strategies as standards or models beneficial for the rebuilding and strengthening of his home country in the future. Wherever he went, Kang Youwei would write down detailed travel accounts, many of which were, out of his regular practice, expressed in the form of poetry. The anthology of Kang Youwei's travel poems collected in this book is only a handful of all the overseas travel poems he wrote, which totaled up to 865 poems. The poems in this anthology were chosen for being among the best in representing Kang's poetic talents, as well as his thoughts, and interests as his journey took him across the world.

Kang Youwei's travel poems are accounts of real journeys and real places in a narrative and lyrical style, in which travel narration, landscape appreciation, and personal sentiments are blended into an organic whole. Before his eyes, foreign landscapes, ancient objects, sculptures, and museums, etc. would immediately instigate a strong poetic urge in him and trigger his homesickness, heartbreak lament on the crushing of China's reform. Worries about his home country's current situation, and his own utter helplessness to do anything to help were forefront. The poet's fantastic imagination, coupled with his talented descriptive language, rendered his poems vividly attractive in scenes and occasions, artistically appealing, and spiritually conforming.

An evident feature noted in Kang Youwei's travel poems was his extensive use of metaphors in the form of historical classics and allusions. The poet's solid mastery of ancient Chinese literature and proficiency in ancient prose endowed him with an ability to have spontaneous and appropriate quotations ready anytime at his fingertips, with which he deftly composed sentences into couplets, apply the past to describe the present, and blend artistic concept with reality. His wide book knowledge of European history, culture and customs also enabled him to use the European "foreignness" and historical happenings and allusions to reflect his thoughts on the prospective of China-west country's encounters. Through his lens as a historian, the poet wrote from his close observation of the social, political and culture aftermath of the war in Europe and then expressed his thoughts and comments, centered about his reform ideology and ultimate goal of making China strong.

Admittedly, the poet's remarkable talent in use of metaphoric ancient Chinese allusions and European historical background renders his poems complex and difficult to most present-day readers. Therefore, the reading circles and critical study of Kang's travel poems have been relatively limited. This anthology of poems, set as a bilingual version in both Chinese and English, aims to promote Kang Youwei's travel poems to ordinary Chinese readers as well as western readers who are interested in China's modern history and reformer Kang Youwei. Anyone, with a basic knowledge of English, will be comfortably able to understand the contents and enjoy the poems through the bridge of translation. The intricate and complex metaphoric ancient allusions, being translated into plain and easy-to-understand English, are surely a good source of learning traditional Chinese literature. The puzzling age-old European historical allusions, being transformed into everyday English, become interesting stories, a fun way to learn European history.

The translation of this book has been done in an attempt to maintain historical facts, convey the true spirit and content of the poet's original work with a necessity to alter style, structure, and grammar from a remote traditional Chinese language to smooth English syntax and idioms. Hopefully this effort creates a lyrical flow and poetic flavor, making poetry reading a source of enjoyment and a great time of learning as well.

Sixteen years of Kang Youwei's life can be concluded with one word "journey" and summarized into a short account of his traveling life as the words on his favorite travel seal shown on this book cover, which reads: "One hundred days of Reform, sixteen years of exile, three world tours, four continents and thirty-one countries visited, six hundred thousand *li* traveled." A born poet, Kang Youwei's poetry has been considered most sophisticated and creative in the Chinese circle of poetry. An unprecedented traveler, he wrote poems from his vast overseas travel experiences that were rich in content, dynamic in language, lyric in style and patriotic in values. The numerous trips he made are, in a sense, trips of culture, trips of history, trips of inner-being's odyssey, turned into poems from his remarkable poetry creativity. They are excellent materials for studying literature, history and Reformer Kang Youwei, a resonance forever echoing with the passing of time in Chinese modern history.

日本

Japan 1898–1899

加拿大

Canada 1899–1904

瑞士

Switzerland 1904

戊戌九月国变出亡，谢上野季三郎领事君相济，康有为赠。

Being forced into exile after the overturning of his Reform Movement of 1898, Kang Youwei received timely help from the Japanese Consul 上野季三郎 (1864–1933) for his personal safety. Kang wrote a poem on a silk scroll for him to show his appreciation.

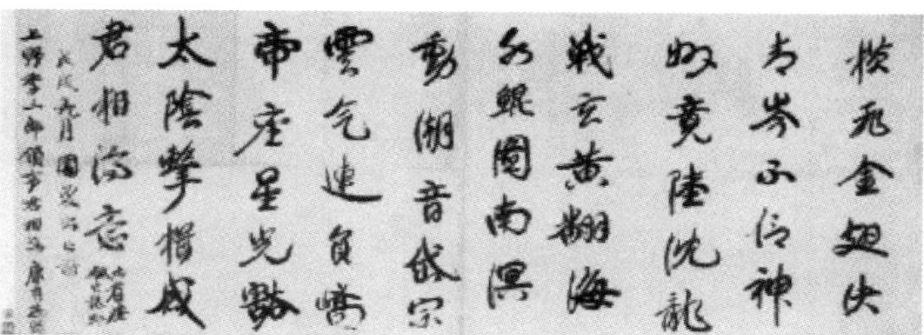

康有为手稿

Kang Youwei's Manuscript

横飞金翅决青岑，不信神州竟陆沉。

龙战玄黄翻海水，鲲图南溟动潮音。

岱宗灵气连员峤，帝座星光豁太阴。

击楫感君相济意，共看腰剑作龙吟。

Its golden wings, alas, crushed unexpectedly to pieces upon the Divine Land.
Yellow dragons, engaged in fierce battles, overturning seas and rivers,
Giant fishes in South Sea brewing changes of the tides.
Spirit of mountain in mainland[1] bonds with celestial mountain overseas[2],
Emperor's constellation starlight exempts moon waning.
Heartfelt gratitude for your kind help with our common goal,
Equipped with a waist sword, we sing songs pledging patriotism.

1 mountain in mainland: Mount Tai in China

2 celestial mountain overseas: Fujiyama in Japan

日本
Japan 1898–1899

加拿大
Canada 1899–1904

瑞士
Switzerland 1904

文岛
Wen Island 1899

中国戊戌变法失败，康有为逃亡海外。在加拿大时，他作诗十九首，内容都和他曾居住过的“文岛”有关。然而康有为并未明确指出文岛是哪一个岛屿，这就成了研究康有为海外史的一个不解之谜。但从康有为的文岛诗、康同璧编写的《南海康先生年谱续编》，以及加拿大国家档案馆的史料中，可以推断出该文岛就是温哥华岛悉尼镇（Sidney, B.C.）以北约 2.5 英里[1]的一个小岛，现名高洁岛（Goudge Island）。

1899 年 4 月，康有为抵达加拿大的维多利亚，当时慈禧太后悬赏十万美金捉拿他。为了躲避刺客，康有为在加拿大居住的半年时间里，前后两次隐居在这个小岛上，每次逗留一两个月。在他居住的简陋卧室里，仅有一张支架床、一张粗木桌和几把椅子。康有为每天花大量时间伏案看书写作。在此期间，康有为写下了《文岛杂咏十九首》，用诗的形式生动地记录下他文岛上的生活点滴。从他的杂咏诗里，读者可以领略一百多年前加拿大海岛的原始文化、

1　英里：英制长度单位，约合 1.6 公里。

生态环境，以及康有为的内心世界。更为重要的是，1899年康有为在文岛期间撰写了《保皇会序文》等一系列保皇会纲领性文献。1904年他再次来到文岛生活时，完成了《物质救国论》《欧洲十一国游记序》等主要著作。

Being driven into exile in 1899, Kang Youwei arrived in Canada and first landed in Victoria. He lived, for over a month, on Wen Island[1], which was located north of Victoria, B.C., to avoid assassination. On the island, Kang wrote a total of nineteen poems in the summer and fall of 1899, recording his life. Kang Youwei lived in a bare upper story of a Canadian wooden house with no furniture besides a trestle bed, a rough pine table, and a couple of chairs. His table was filled with Chinese books. On that desk, Kang spent a lot of time writing and finished some important pieces of work, including "*Introduction to the Charter of the Chinese Reform Association*[2]". In 1904 when he was back to live on Wen Island, he completed quite a few of his major works, such as: *The Theory of Saving the Nation by Materials* and *Preface to An Observation Tour of Eleven European Countries*, etc.

---

1 Wen Island refers to today's Goudge Island, which is close to Swartz Bay Ferry terminal, British Columbia.

2 Chinese Reform Association is the same as Baohuanghui (Protect Emperor Association).

文岛杂咏十九首 己亥夏秋

Miscellaneous Wen Island Poems Written in Summer/Fall of 1899

俯瞰高洁岛和魏泗岛，2019

Aerial view of Goudge Island and Coal Island, Courtesy of John Adams, Victoria, B.C. 2019

流离已久，忧病头风。此海千岛，雪山照人。日游一岛，始居帐幕，继装潢渔室，名曰“寥天”。前后两居凡弥月。志士冯俊卿奔走供给，护卫至周。

Being driven into exile for a long while, afflicted by a heart down, a headache persistent. Thousands of islands stand in this sea, white and bright, snow mountains shine.

Daytime touring to an island, nighttime lodging in a tent.

Renovation of the house has been under way, I named it “Liao Tian Haven”[1]. In the house I lived for two periods apart. For a whole month, Comrade Feng[2] stayed busy, in full charge of my safety and daily needs.

---

1 Liao Tian Haven：寥天室。

2 Feng：Feng Junqing（冯俊卿），a Chinese living in Victoria, a close comrade of Kang.

其一

域多利海岛无数，山离雉泊我来游。

每日荡舟游一岛，夕阳醉绕魏家洲。

Countless islands in Victoria,
In mountains, pheasant's habitat, a tourist I come.
Riding a boat daily to an islet.
In dusk, drunk, going around Wei Si Island[1] home.

1 Wei Si Island, a small island named by Kang, because his friend Wei Si lived there.

其二

哀歌击楫气纵横，珠岛周遭带醉行。
惊起前洲渔者识，依稀故国棹歌声。

Drumming the boat, singing in high spirit,
Going around Pearl Island, drunk.
Catching attention of a fisherman, a friend of mine,
Homeland's melody echoing faintly in the ear.

其三

小岛周遭十顷余，小山松柏满幽居。
坐收平果生涯足，牧豕屠羊更取鱼。

The small island stretches for ten hectares.
A multitude of pines, cedars, and secluded
houses fill the hills.
Raising pigs, herding sheep, and catching fish,
Produce abundant, life on the island is rich.

其四

日日矶头坐看潮，长眠石上树萧萧。

苍苔寸厚无人到，但有鸭声破寂寥。

Sitting at a jet head everyday,
watching tide changing,
Lying long on a rock,
listening to trees' brisk singing.
Path untrodden,
covered with moss, green and thick,
Random quacks of ducks break the silence.

其五

大海网鱼新事业，深山砍木好工夫。

新来学得操舟法，日向烟波作画图。

Sea fishing's a fresh thing to do,
Cutting wood in forest now my piece of cake.
Boat sailing, a skill I newly acquired,
Facing smoky waves, I draw pictures.

其六

居帐还同游牧国，秋千拣得大松林。

有人来觅明夷[1]子，丛木崇冈深更深。

Living in a tent as if touring in a nomadic country,
Exploring the whole pine forest to find spot for
a swing.
If somebody tries to find me here,
Only to find woods deep, bushes dense.

1 明夷：康有为，号长素，又号明夷、更生。

其七

午时泳浴海波中，冰雪肌肤对冷风。
旁人问我冷何许，对面雪山初雪溶。

Swimming in the sea at noon,
Freezing body against cold wind.
Being asked how cold do I feel,
As the mountain snow just starting to melt.

其八

牵萝补屋缀山斋，老木荒僵作几排。

上有松枝阴最绿，读书孤坐浪湝湝。

Threadbare house simple and shabby,
Aged coarse wood laid in rows.
Pine trees shade well overhead,
Reading and writing all by myself,
Sound of waves my constant company.

其九

晚来绕岛一周遭，隐处看云更听涛。

穿树欹崖犹未了，险浔深处试三篙。

Evening boat rounding the island,
In the hideout, watching clouds changing,
Listening to waves humming.
Along the cliffs, passing under the tree branches,
Punting the boat wherever water is deep,
Once, once more and more.

其十

老柏苍僵大十围，忽遭野火对斜晖。

异香十日烧难尽，观我生兮何所归。

An aged cypress tree, its trunk gigantic,
Can't be encircled even by ten persons' joined arms.
Caught on fire all of a sudden,
Fire light against sunset glow.
Lasting for ten days,
Exotic rosin permeating the air.
Occurred to my mind was the question:
Whom should I give allegiance to?

其十一

回首中原叹陆沉，兵缠大角气森森。

老夫短褐登场猎，日日校枪能中心。

Thinking of the lost territory of my motherland,
Invading military staring,
wanting to devour all her land.
Old bones in a brown short jacket,
Drill everyday, able to hit the center of a target.

其十二

黄松岛大多野鸡，校猎幽寻山路迷。

深林苍翠暮烟紫，穿出矶头看日西。

Pheasants are numerous on Yellow Pine Island,
Hunting in the mountain, lost our way.
Forest deep and green, twilight smoke purple,
Head reaching out of the jet head,
Looking for the sunset direction in the west.

其十三

海底齿齿沙石见，海面青青荇带舒。

系舟倒挂岸松下，卧看渔人网截鱼。

Teeth-like sand stones clear at the sea bottom,
Sparse green seaweeds floating softly on the sea.
Fastening the boat vertically under a pine tree,
Reclining on a rock, I watch fishermen net fishing.

其十四

石斑鱼美世所无，椰菜数畦香异殊。

邻家开网朝朝送，天遗土产不须租。

Grouper fish, king of the delicacy,
Cabbage fresh from the field delicious.
Neighboring fishermen bring fish everyday,
Naturally grown produce, no need to pay.

其十五

瑶台怪石暮跻攀，蘅杜江花满石斑。

老柏奇松低入海，卧悬树杪听潺潺。

Outside my haven,
various rocks look more bizarre in dusk,
Covered all over by grass thick and flower blooming.
Old cedars and pines rooting ashore crawling
into the sea,
Treetops leaning inclined,
listening to the gurgle of the sea.

其十六

八月十三日，与志士刘康恒、李福基祭六烈士于寥天室。

On Lunar August 13, 1899, Kang Youwei and two comrades commemorated six martyrs killed in the Reform Movement of 1898, including his own brother Kang Guangren (康广仁).

殊方穷发寥天室，痛哭英灵赋大招。
西望瀛台波渺渺，逋臣洒涕满江潮。

In the Liao Tian Haven,
a far-flung place from the world,
Weeping bitterly for the souls lost in the heroic cause.
Looking west through cloudy waves towards Yingtai[1],
Tears flow quick, pouring into the river,
swelling its tide.

1 Yingtai, the place that Emperor Guangxu was kept in confinement.

其十七

海云海浪两冥冥，秋气秋心不敢醒。

尽日头风医不得，海波沐我月华生。

Sea clouds, sea waves, unfathomable,

Autumn weather, autumn heart, dare not to wake.

Lingering headache gets no cure,

Bathing in sea waves, heart soothed.

其十八

思君念母客万里，忧国怀人又九秋。

最是痛心当八月，经年须发白盈头。

Missing friends, thinking of mother,
Thousands of miles away, I'm stranded.
Worrying about my people and homeland,
Autumn returns.
Last August[1] hurts me most,
In one year, gray hair hastened to turn white.

1 Last August refers to the Reform Movement of 1898 in China which was crushed bloodily by the conservative force headed by Empress Dowager Cixi（慈禧）.

其十九

申胥[1]痛哭知何往，正则[2]行吟更自伤。

万里投荒住孤岛，登山临水总凄凉。

Shen Xu[3] wept bitterly,

knowing where he's heading for,

Walking aimlessly,

Zhengze[4] recited poems, Only hurting the self more.

Taking flight to this island of isolation,

Roaming among mountains and waters,

My heart always heavy in desolation.

---

1 申胥：申包胥哭秦庭借兵。

2 正则：屈原，自云名正则，在沅江江畔，边行边吟《渔父》词，以示心情忧愤苦闷。

3 Shen Xu, a historic figure went to Country Qin（秦国）and cried out bitterly, asking for their military help.

4 Zhengze, another name of Chinese ancient poet Qu Yuan（屈原）.

康有为的另外几首文岛诗

Kang Youwei's other poems written on Wen Island

己亥六月十三日，与义士李福基、冯秀石及子俊卿、徐为经、骆月湖、刘康恒等创立保皇会。于二十八日，至域多利中华会馆，率邦人恭祝圣寿，龙旗摇扬，观者如云。湾高华与二埠同日举行。海外祝嘏自此始也。

BHH (Baohuanghui, Protect the Emperor Society) was founded on July 20, 1899. On August 4, 1899, BHH held a grand birthday celebration for Emperor Guangxu（光绪）who had been put under house arrest in Yingtai（瀛台）, Beijing.

恭祝圣寿 己亥六月二十八日

海外初瞻寿域开，龙旂披拂白楼台。
白人碰盏掎裳至，黄种然灯夹巷来。
上帝与龄怜下土，小臣泣拜倒蒿莱。
遥从文岛瞻琼岛，波绕瀛台梦几回。

Celebration of Emperor's Birthday

From overseas, birthday congratulations pour in,
On the white veranda[1], dragon flags flutter.
Crowds of white people cheer with wine,
In alleys, flows of yellow people holding
lanterns high.
Blessed am I by His Majesty's grace,
Humbled, tears in eyes,
I bowed down as the reach of Penghao[2] falling
to the ground.
From Wen Island, I look into the distant Yingtai Island[3],
Crossing waters and lands,
Meeting with Majesty in dream repeats times again.

---

1 White verandarefers to the building of Chinese Benevolent Association in Victoria.

2 Penghao, name of wild grass, weed.

3 Yingtai refers to the small island of Zhongnanhai in Beijing, where Emperor Guangxu was imprisoned.

文岛仲秋夜，有故乡苏村之苏熠来陪，与话故乡事惘然，写付寄乡人。

On Mid-Moon Festival in 1899, a friend named Su Yi from home Su Village paid a visit to Kang Youwei on Wen Island to accompany him for the festival. They talked about their hometown and bygone days. Su asked Kang to write him a letter to the folks in their village, so Kang wrote the following poem and sent it to Su.

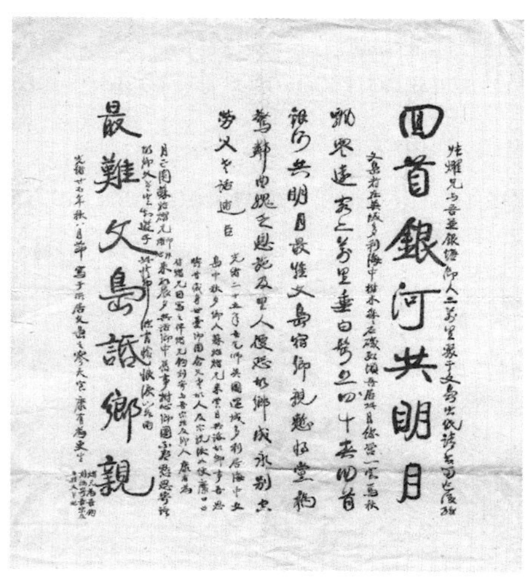

康有为《文岛仲秋夜》诗手稿

Kang Youwei's Manuscript of Mid-Moon Festival

文岛仲秋夜

飘零远客二万里，垂白鬓丝四十春。

回首银河共明月，最难文岛话乡亲。

惭将党祸惊邻曲，愧乏恩施及里人。

便恐故乡成永别，空劳父老话逋臣。

Moon Festival on Wen Island

Wandering afar twenty thousand *li*,

Gray temples, forty years of age telling.

Remembering the good old days,

Enjoying bright moon with friends.

Rarely comes a friend from home,

To stay overnight with me.

Havoc from the parties' battle, guilt's mine,

Powerless to repay the friends, guilt's mine.

Lest my homeland's a forever farewell,

In exile, my sincere apology to my people at home.

游魏泗岛，其妇以瓜见赠 1899. 9. 20

小滩咽咽树幽幽，独木为桥过隔洲。

野雉争飞瓜正熟，夕阳孤岛荡轻舟。

A Trip to Wei Si[1] Island

Small beach gloomy, thick woods shady,
A single-plank bridge, connecting east with west.
Pheasants flying and puffing,
ripened melons pleasing,
Paddling a canoe home from the lonely island in dusk.

1 Wei Si Island refers to the Coal Island today. Kang Youwei's friend Wei Si (魏泗) rented a piece of land on the island and lived there. Therefore, Kang named it Wei Si Island. Wei's wife on the island gave Kang some melons to please him.

游魏岛归棹，望海思家，时太夫人及眷属住澳门。

璧月亭亭出海边，远山近岛紫凝烟。

踊跃金轮海山碧，遥知濠镜影同圆。

Back from the trip to Wei Si Island, I watch the sea, missing home, Mother Madam Lao[1], wife and relatives living in Macao.

Elegant moon emerging from the sea,
Mountains afar, islands close, in purple smoke set.
Golden wheel flying,
passing through mountains and waters,
News from remote Macao,
reuniting us in full moon's circle.

1 Mother Madam Lao: Kang Youwei's mother (劳太夫人).

1899 年 10 月 1 日，康有为惜别文岛和他的寥天室，作诗《别文岛》。

Having lived on Wen Island for over a month, Kang Youwei had established a close rapport with the place and his house which he named Liao Tian Haven. Before his departure, Kang wrote a poem, expressing his deep feelings.

别文岛 1899. 10. 1

别文岛，周游之，跌足而返，回望吾庐寥天室，怅然不忍舍去。

岛树别离行一周，沙滩跌足不能游。

兴澜缘尽从兹去，归棹回头独倚舟。

文岛幽居占月余，风烟草树不吾疏。

天涯走遍佳山水，比似寥天总不如。

Bye to Wen Island

Before leaving the island, I wandered around,

Hurting my foot in the sand, unable to walk further. No more leaning on the rails in leisure.

Home-bound boat moored alone in port.

Having lived in seclusion one month and more,

Wind and fog, tree and grass,

All to me, dear memories to be cherished.

Beautiful landscape all over the world,

No rival for my Liao Tian Haven on the island.

甲辰十月二十九日重游加拿大域多利之文岛，徘徊寥天室故宅。

Kang Youwei returned to his Liao Tian Haven on Wen Island in 1904. These two poems he wrote then have never been published before. Pacing in the room of Liao Tian Haven, Kang Youwei wrote the following lines on December 5, 1904, five years after he left the house.

文岛重移棹，凄凉觅故居。
海山仍缥缈，林木尚扶疏。
门栅倾斜矣，园墙尚晏如。
经过五年梦，京邑已邱墟。
再入寥天室，凝尘房榻虚。
山松犹户外，万木尚庭余。
屋瓦低无恙，池畦亦太初。
颇怀苏武节，北海有毡庐。
环岛周遭步，摩挲故物迁。
屿边安几榻，松上挂秋千。
重眠听海浪，复坐啸风烟。
穿入深林路，苔痕似昔年。

Back to Wen Island,
heart hurt to find the old house bleak,
As before, sea and mountains surreal,
forest trees flourishing.
Patio door frame tilts, door leans,
Walls remain upright.
As what had occurred in my dreams for five years,
The capital city's fallen into ruin.
Inside Liao Tian Haven,
House in dust, bed quaking.
Outside, mountain pines still stand tall,
Woods still lavishing.
House tiles laid low, no danger looming,
Pounds trimly framed by dikes no change.
Reminiscing Su Wu's[1] patriotism,
Holding him fast in yurt in North Sea.
Wandering around the island,
Fondling the old stuff all over.
Placing couches on the edge of the island,
Hanging a swing on a pine tree.

1 Su Wu（苏武）, a historic steadfast patriot who, driven by starvation in the north, ate camel hair from yurt for survival.

Lulled by soothing sea waves, sleep comes,
Lying on couch, wind whistling into ear.
Walking through into the forest,
Moss thick as old days.

海山飘渺曾经住

海山缥缈曾经住，风浪纵横亦出游；
旧国风云已桑海，故居邱壑尚松楸。
苍茫岛屿犹能认，激荡波涛未得休；
树石岂知再摩抚，五年万叹一环球。

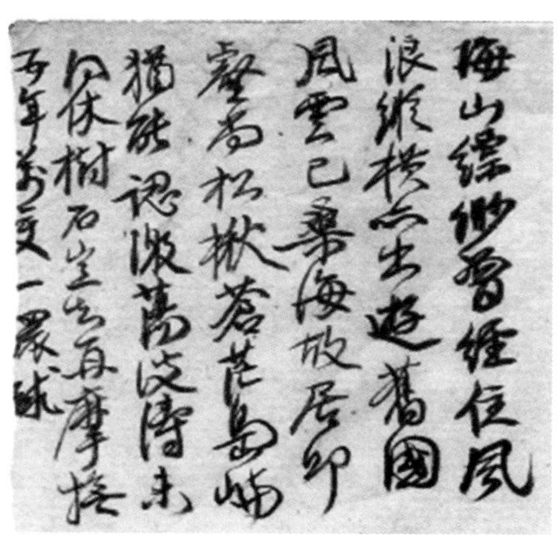

康有为手稿《海山缥缈曾经住》(作者收藏)
On this Dream-like earth of sea and mountains,
I once lived Kang youwei's Manuscript (Collected by Author)

On this dream-like earth of sea and mountains,
I once lived,
Strong wind and big waves propel distant sailing.
Gone with the sea are the bygones in motherland,
Ancestral tombs in hometown were destroyed.
The island, hazy though, looks familiar,
Rapid and tall waves slow down not a bit.
Trees and rocks not knowing that's my caressing,
The passing of five years saw me touring
around the world,
Heard me heaving sighs thousands of times.

湾高华[1]

Vancouver 1904

1904 年，康有为再度来到温哥华。当时保皇会已迅速发展到五大洲，160 多个分会，其管理资金筹措等方方面面的工作量巨大；加美两地的反华浪潮日益高涨；中国正面临庚子赔款和被列强瓜分的紧张局势。这些使康有为忧心忡忡，身心疲惫到体力不支，咽喉疼痛失声。故前去新建的北温哥华旅馆避会访客，静心休息，并着力完成一些重要著作。康有为作诗两首，写下了他去北温旅馆途中的所见所闻。

1 现译为“温哥华”。

In 1904, Kang Youwei went to Vancouver again. Having been under a tremendous amount of pressure from the management of over 160 Baohuanghui branches all over the world, the rising tide of anti-China sentiment in North America, the dire situation that China was facing after signing "Final Protocol for the Settlement of the Disturbances of 1900", Kang Youwei became physically weak and lost his voice due to a severe sore throat. To better recuperate as well as concentrate on writing, Kang Youwei went to stay in a newly built hotel in North Vancouver. He wrote two poems about what he saw on the way to that hotel.

病卧湾高华

山泽浪游，地多僵木，皆数千年，烧之以辟人居，板桥四通，行之无尽。甲辰十一月

板桥石濑溜溅溅，临水山花亦妙妍。

行遍荒山看野烧，荒僵巨木尽千年。

Bedridden in Vancouver December

Wandering among mountains and rivers, seeing everywhere has been disturbed with dead trees, fallen limbs, aged a thousand years. To be burnt and cleaned up for the development of residential areas. Plank bridges stretch in all directions, paths approaching in endless ways.

Under the plank bridges,
Shallow water dashing and splashing,
Wildflowers around budding and blooming.
Roaming all over the barren mountains,
Watching the wildfire burning,
Giant trees extinguished,
lost after a thousand years.

湾高华对海旅店夜步 甲辰十一月

海夜波涛拍岸粗，冷风吹月渡明湖。

步从烟剪巢边过，大雪封山万树枯。

注：美洲土人名曰烟剪，盖印度转也，华人呼其厦曰巢。

Night Walk Around North Vancouver Hotel

Harsh night waves lapping the shores,
Cold gusts pushing the moon across Vancouver Harbor.
Passing through the Indian quarter,
Mountains are covered with snow, all trees withered.

Note: The natives of North America are Indians whose name is from the country India.

北温哥华旅馆（建于 1902 年）
Hotel North Vancouver（built in 1902）

哈里森温泉
Harrison Hot Springs 1904

1899 年 4 月，流亡海外的康有为初到温哥华，一直被头痛病所困扰。听说山中有一处拥有丰富碳酸的温泉——嬉理慎温泉，今称哈里森温泉（Harrison Hot Springs），可以治病，于是前往小住数日，泡温泉治病，并享受那里得天独厚的美景。哈里森温泉位于美丽的哈里森湖（Harrison Lake）之滨，距离温哥华 130 余公里。

加拿大太平洋铁路的开通使交通更为便利，康有为在本地华人温金有、刘康恒等人的陪同下，从新西敏（New Westminster）乘火车到厄紧士（Agassiz）。从车站到哈里森湖的两边都是茂密的原始森林，当地人砍树开发了一条小通道，直达哈里森湖畔的圣·爱丽丝旅店（St. Alice Hotel）。康有为一行就下榻在那个酒店。

1904 年底，康有为再次来到哈里森温泉，仍住圣·爱丽丝旅店。正逢一场大雪过后，康有为赋诗记录下当时的所见所闻。康有为乘坐火车到希望小镇（Hope），然后沿着诗中的“鸟阁道”(Nicola Trail）步行进入考奎哈拉河（Coquihalla River）的峡谷地区。如今“鸟阁道”已经荡然无存了，因为 1912 年起铺建的一条 KVR 铁路，在花岗岩的山体上开凿了五段隧道，彻底改变了原来道路的走向，因此地图上就没有任何 Nicola Trail 的标记可寻了。据说，当年康有为听说当地政府要在这样复杂的地形中建铁路，并且已经开始进行勘测，很是新奇，决心要到此地看个究竟。从诗中，可以了解到当时的“鸟阁道”是在半山或者山顶上，才有“翠崖劈两峙，绿水泻中流”的美景。

哈里森温泉和哈里森湖（远处桥边为圣•爱丽丝旅店）
Harrison Hot Springs, and Harrison Lake, B. C.

圣·爱丽丝旅店草坪 St. Alice Hotel on the lawn

Harrison Hot Springs

In April of 1899, Kang Youwei in exile first arrived in Vancouver. He had been afflicted with a severe headache for a long while. Having learned there was a hot mineral spring in Harrison whose water had a high sulfuric concentration with good healing effect, he decided to go there for a couple of days to enjoy the warm spring and heal. The spring was located alongside the Harrison River with a distance of approximately 130 kilometers away from Vancouver.

The opening of the Canadian Pacific Railway brought the lakeside springs within a short carriage ride of the transcontinental mainline. Accompanied by several Chinese Canadian friends, Kang Youwei took a train from New Westminster to Agassiz. On both sides of the railway there were lush forests. From the Agassiz railway station, there was a road leading into the thick woods. The local people cut down trees and opened up a direct path from the railway station to St. Alice Hotel, where Kang Youwei stayed.

At the end of 1904, Kang Youwei came again to Harrison Hot Spring and stayed at the same hotel. He took a train to a small town named Hope, then walked Nicola Trail and entered the Coquihalla River area. Today that Nicola Trail no longer exists, because of the building of KVR railway in 1912. It was said that Kang Youwei, having heard of the railway construction proposal in such a complex terrain, he, out of curiosity, made a special trip to the place to take a look. Hence the writing of the following poem from which the beautiful Nicola scene can be seen:

Green cliff chopped apart into two sides,

In between, mountain water racing down in a green flow.

重游嬉理慎温泉，宿故店 甲辰十一月

重山伐木深通道，山尽途穷见水明。

廿里烟波开妩媚，万杉楼阁对澄清。

岭巅雪影兼云影，桥畔泉声与浪声。

再循磴道摩林石，虽酌温泉已冷成。

Revisiting Harrison Hot Springs, Staying in the Same St. Alice Hotel

In deep woods,
a logging path extends far,
Reaching its end,
rolling mountains stop,
clean water comes into view.
Stretching for twenty miles,
charming waves open warm arms,
Mirrored fir trees in multitude,
edifices on the bank.
On the mountaintop,
snow merges with the clouds in the sky,

Under the bridge,
spring water chorusing with sound of the waves.
Climbing the stone steps,
touching the forest stones,
Drinking,
enjoying the cooled down water in the hot spring.

嬉理慎温泉看大雪，与林铎[1]湖溪泛

甲辰十一月

野月荒荒暗，松林杳杳冥。
群峰皆雪色，万壑带泉声。
僵木纵横倒，溪流曲折清。
白凫同呷喋，打桨一无惊。

横云藏岛屿，大雪漏林丘。
溪小成专制，湖深得自由。
波高扬岬滐，天大听沉浮。
泛泛原无住，行行任自休。

再过鸟阁道，海峡最深幽。
翠崖劈两峙，绿水泻中流。
雪岭看无已，飞泉听不休。
苔钱封巨石，人迹少来游。

1　林铎，康有为弟子，保皇会资助的留学生之一，1904—1905 年时正在温哥华求学。

Watching Big Snow in Harrison Hot Spring and Boating in a Lake with Lin Duo[1]

The moon in the wilderness dim and dull,
Pine forest creepy and gloomy.
Mountain peaks, under the cloak of snow, all white,
Valleys humming, echoing the sound of spring.
Fallen trees lie crisscross on the ground,
Stream water runs zigzag in a clear flow.
White birds, singing in chorus,
While boats passing, their singing
uninterrupted.

Crossing clouds hiding islands,
Snowfall missing some hills.
Water running, guided by the small stream's flow,
Into the deep lake, freedom obtained.
Waves, rolling up and flapping at the dikes,
Making big noises in the vast open.
A wild place with no residence,

1 Lin Duo, Kang's disciple.

Everything lives or dies on its own.

Passing again the Nicola Trail,
The deepest of the strait[1].
Green cliff chopped apart into two sides,
In between, mountain water racing down in a green flow.
Never enough is the view of the snow-topped mountains,
Never enough is the pleasing music of the springs.
Colossal rocks sealed with thick moss,
Paths untrodden by human steps.

鸟阁道下的涧水

The Canyon of the Coquihalla River, Hope, British Columbia

1 The strait refers to the canyon of the Coquihalla River, Hope, British Columbia.

加拿大
Canada 1899–1904

地中海
Mediterranean 1904

意大利
Italy 1904

瑞士
Switzerland 1904

法国
France 1904

1903年10月，康有为至香港省母。迫于严峻的形势，他仍不得久留。在陪母亲过完春节后，康不得已于1904年3月再次启程远游，5月抵达槟榔屿。短暂歇脚后，便乘英轮自槟榔屿启程，前往欧洲。

In October 1903, Kang Youwei went to Hong Kong to take care of his mother. He was unable to stay long under the circumstances. Having spent Chinese Spring Festival together with his mother, he had to take leave. Heaving sighs, he decided on making a trip to Europe in March 1904.

将为汗漫[1]游，去港别亲三首，甲辰二月六日（选一首）

地狱欣然入，来因救众生。

怵心虽苦戒，乘愿亦何惊。

悲悯开新世，庄严起化城。

诸天无去住，且听海潮声。

On March 22, 1904, Kang Youwei bid farewell to his family and friends in Hong Kong before his departure for a long journey. He wrote three poems about it.

Entering hell with no regrets,
Because it's for the purpose of saving my people.
Living a life in danger no doubt a terrible retribution,
Fighting for a cause noble and just,
I'll fear no evil.
A solemn new world unfolding before me,
A fantasy mirage in grave hallucination.
Nowhere can be called home on all of the earth,
Only listening to sound from the lapping of waves.

1 形容漫游之远，远游。

锡兰乘孖摩拉[1]巨舰往欧洲，新睹巨制，目为耸然。

渡海至锡兰，巍巍睹巨舰。
楼观四五层，俯临沧波澹。
惊飞上云表，鹏翼九天鉴。
其长六十丈，洞廊窗深堑。
千室以容客，弘廓尤泛滥。
重过一万吨，结构森惨淡。
巨浪拍如山，邈若蚍蜉撼。
惊波了无觉，蹈海若枕簟。
信兹楼舰力，能故海石陷。
昔称万斛船[2]，北人信不敢。
今乃廿倍过，后者应难勘。
浮海突奇峰，岛屿筑天堑。
眼前突兀见此船，海不扬波无险探。

1　孖摩拉（Marmara），船名。
2　万斛船，很大的船只。

I first arrived at Penang Island, and after a short stay, I took the British passenger ship Marmara heading for Europe. I was stunned seeing for the first time such a colossal ship.

Coming to Sri Lanka via a sea passage way,
Before my eyes was a colossal passenger ship.
It's structure dull and gloomy,
It's cargo capacity over ten thousand tons.
When sailing she looked as if flying,
With massive wings riding wind into the clouds.
Her body sixty *zhang*[1] in length,
Hallways extending in deep and secluded ends.
Hundreds of cabins holding thousands,
Substantial capacity allowing overflow of people.
Her weight over ten thousand ton,
Her structure dull and gloomy.
Firm as mountain when being slapped against
by breakers,
Like ants trying to shake a giant tree.
Feeling safe when sailing on bumpy and rough waters,
Feeling steady on sea like sleeping on pillow at home.
Having a full trust in the ship's capability,

1 *zhang*: Chinese measurement in length, one *zhang* = 3.33 meter

Not worrying about personal safety at all.
In old days, largest cargo ship was called Wanhu ship,
Which were beyond Northerners' ken.
Twenty times more powerful is this ship,
It's capacity almost impossible for people to believe.
Grotesque peaks thrusting towards the sky,
Islands and islets forming natural chasms.
The gigantic ship emerging before me all of a sudden,
The sea remaining peaceful tossing no waves or storms.

越六年己酉六月，自伦敦再乘此船还，则见此船卑小，画设皆恶，船则犹是，吾见大非，盖六年久游欧美，心目化之，非复故吾矣。

地中海歌（节选）

滔滔洪波，邈邈天幕。

几世之雄，赋诗横槊。

汽船如飞，我今过兹。

浊浪排天，浩浩淘之。

英迹杳杳，犹在书诗。

地中海之人民秀白，

地中海之山岳华离。

激荡变化，颇难测知。

全球但见海环地，岂有万里大海在地中之恢奇。

地形诡异吾地稀，宜其众国之竞峙而雄立，

日新而妙微。

昨日一日行希腊，云峰耸秀天表接。

岛屿万千曲曲穿，澜漪绿碧翻翻涉。

遥望雅典、哥林多[1]，岚霭溟蒙岳巀嵲。

七贤不可见，民政今未渫。

呜呼文明出地形，谁纵天骄此洴渫。

1 今译作“科林斯”(Corinth)，也叫哥林多，位于伯罗奔尼撒半岛的东北，临科林斯湾，是希腊本土和伯罗奔尼撒半岛的连接点。

Six years afterwards in July 1907, I retook the ship on my way back. I found, to my surprise, that the ship appeared much smaller and different now, interior design in paintings and displays both ugly and grotesque. I have been traveling in Europe for six years, the experience of which has broadened my horizon and vision a great deal.

Song of Mediterranean

Surging sea waves rolling on,
Vault of heaven in distant sky.
Heroes of the eras,
Writing poems remarkably imposing.
Steamship sailing as if flying,
In which I ride with scenes swiftly passing.
Waves and breakers forming a choppy sea,
Running forward in a formidable array.
Heroic deeds gone with the wind,
Alive only in books and verses.
Mediterranean people honest and innocent,
Mediterranean mountains grand and majestic.
Turbulent changes all of a sudden,

No one, alas, was able to foretell.
Of the whole earth, sea enclosing land not uncommon geography,
Yet sea enclosed by land is for sure uncommon.
Weird landform and irregular terrains,
Each Mediterranean country standing in sovereignty in its own territory,
Unaware of subtle changes with the passing of time.
I stopped at Greece yesterday for a visit,
Amazed at lofty mountain peaks soaring into clouds.
Thousands of islets standing entwined with each other,
In green water rippling with the wind.
Looking at Athens and Corinth from afar,
Shrouded in mountain mist and drizzling haze.
Seven noble sages not yet to be seen,
Civil administration not yet to be born.
Calling out, alas, for civilization to be realized,
Who'll be in heavenly control of this turbulence!

加拿大
Canada 1899–1904

地中海
Mediterranean 1904

意大利
Italy 1904

瑞士
Switzerland 1904

法国
France 1904

1904 年 6 月 15 日，康有为登陆意大利布林迪西，次日一早便转乘火车前往意大利南部第一大城市那不勒斯，在那里他看到他心目中的英雄——统一意大利王国的首任首相加富尔的雕像，将其与诸葛亮相比，有感而发，赋诗一首。

On June 15, 1904, Kang Youwei first set foot in Brindisi, Italy. Early next morning, he took a train to Napoli, there he came across the bronze monument of Camillo Benso, Count of Cavour, the first Premier in Italy who united the nation, whom Kang likewise compared to Zhuge Liang (诸葛亮), a wise military man and skillful strategist of war during the Three Kingdoms period (220–280 AD) in ancient China. Kang's admiration for Cavour was so great that he wrote an elegant poem in dedication to his hero.

我生遍数欧洲才，意相嘉侯实第一。

我今首登欧洲陆，初游即见嘉侯铜像耸云而突兀。

方面大耳修干躯，眉宇雄伟态强倔。

森然天人姿，降诞救意国。

我生最想慕之英雄，忽尔遇之喜舞不可遏。

譬如好色者见所爱慕之美人，情意欢欣中畅发。

忽念构造遇之艰，耸然起敬手加额。

少日躬耕类南阳，壮能择主同诸葛[1]。

君臣鱼水亦复同，明良千古难遇合。

当时革命民主论纷纭，独以尊王违俗说。

遂以分裂十一邦，竟能统一国独立。

外结英、法两君相，内容加、玛二豪杰[2]。

前拒强奥之奴制，后绝霸法相侵压。

成功虽同俾斯麦[3]，艰难缔构过千百。

---

1 诸葛，即诸葛亮，中国古代杰出的政治家、军事家、改革家，以足智多谋闻名。

2 加、玛，即加里波第（Giuseppe Garibaldi）、马志尼（Giuseppe Mazzini），为意大利统一运动豪杰。

3 俾斯麦是德国近代史上一位著名的政治家和外交家，人称“铁血宰相”。南德四邦加入德意志联邦帝国，俾斯麦任宰相。

超然若无人世欲，意国为妻情何窄。

大地嘉耦汝最奇，得此丈夫种不灭。

瓣香我只为公焚，今日相见情弥亲。

有若公生咤风云，挥斥天地独立军。

仗剑昂首问仓旻，微公谁归无典坟。

奈波里本非公国，铸金乃记范蠡[1]勋。

林木森蔚楼台新，海浪淙淙石堤滨。

电灯万千歌乐喧，绣幄香鞋草成茵，

士女嬉游瞻仰频。

我生东方之大秦[2]，当公立国之始已四旬，

与公相隔三万里之关津。

岂意入境第一日，先见公像结缘因。

东海西海波澜接，徘徊怅望想千春。

---

1 范蠡，中国春秋时代的政治家、军事家。

2 大秦，中国史书称罗马帝国（公元前44年）的前身罗马共和国（公元前181年）为“大秦”，所以我中国之秦朝立国时（公元前221年），比罗马共和国的“大秦”立国时早了四十载。

Among all the geniuses of my generation in Europe,
Italian Minister Cavour surely topped the list.
Setting foot on the soil of Europe today,
The bronze monument of Cavour caught my eyes right away.
Towering high in the clouds,
A square face, large ears, wide forehead, and a muscular body.
A majestic figure, born to be the savior of Italy,
The hero I admire most, there he was,
I should have met him accidentally.
Like a lover meeting his dream beauty,
Delight overflowing the heart.
Hit by a thought of the extreme hard work to build such a stunning monument,
I placed a hand to my forehead in salute.
A farmer in his youth,
Growing up to be a counselor assisting the King of Sardinia,
Serving like China's Zhuge[1].
Between wise Majesty and resourceful subject,

1 Zhuge was a resourceful politician, military strategist and reformer in Chinese ancient time.

A fine cooperation led to a victory incredible.
Among dissonant opinions about revolution and democracy,
Only one vision, respecting common interests, proved invincible.
Eleven divided states were finally united as an independent country,
With the aid of Britain and France,
And with the needed help of Garibaldi and Mazzini.[1]
Slavery to the Austro-Hungarian Empire was put to end,
Invasion from France was made impossible.
The success was similar to that of Bismarck[2],
Yet in reality a thousand times harder.
A decent man with no worldly desire,
Holding Italy dear as a wife.
A spouse like you nowhere to be found,
The continuation of the race was guaranteed.
O, for you only, I burn petal incense,
Meeting you today has brought us ever closer.
What a super power,

---

1 Giuseppe Garibaldi, Giuseppe Mazzini were two heroic figures in the movement of the unification of Italy.

2 Bismarck was an important politician and diplomat in German modern history.

Riding whirlwind and shaking heaven and earth!
Watching you holding head high and a sword in hand,
A bond of like-mindedness overwhelmed me.
Napoli's not a state capital,
Yet a monument was founded for your memory
as was for China's hero Fan Li[1].
The foliage thick and green,
and the terraces newly built,
Sea waves singing,
and lapping on the shores.
Thousands of lamps lit,
Hilarious songs and music filling the air.
Embroidered tents,
Elegant shoes dancing on grass velvet green,
Frequent gazing at the monument in respect.
I was born in the Qin Empire[2] in the east,
A lapse of forty years since the foundation of the Roman Empire.
A sea route of thirty-thousand *li* between us,

1 Fan Li was a prominent politician and military strategist in China's Spring and Autumn Period.

2 *Da Qin Empire* refers to Roman Republic (181 BC) which was the predecessor of Rome Empire (44 BC). Therefore, when the Qin Dynasty of China was founded (221 BC), it was 40 years before the founding of the "Da Qin" of the Roman Republic.

What a wonder I met you the first day of my arrival in Italy,
A destined date it must be!
The waves of the eastern sea connecting with the western sea,
My thought, lost in the sea,
Wondering desolately far and wide in time.

意大利王国首相加富尔的塑像
Camillo Benso, Count of Cavour, Bronze Monument in Italy

罗马

Rome 1904

康有为于6月19日上午8时离开那不勒斯，下午3时抵达罗马，入住距离梵蒂冈不远的十九世纪末罗马城最著名的豪华酒店之一的格兰大酒店，于6月26日离开。在罗马的七天里，他陆续凭吊了古罗马帝国许多遗迹，还买了一些纪念品。

Kang Youwei left Naples around 8 am on June 19 and arrived at Rome at 3 pm. He stayed in Grand Hotel Palace Plaza, which was one of the most luxurious hotels in the 19th century. The location was close to the Vatican, allowing easy access and proximity to local attractions and sights. During seven days of his stay there, Kang visited a lot of relics from Roman Empire and purchased some souvenirs.

罗马格兰大酒店

Grand Hotel Palace Plaza

游罗马京，古寺古殿遍地，皆二千年断墙坏瓦，感赋。

七冈草树绿茫茫，大地山河此最伤。
百里石渠连碧汉，千年古道黯斜阳。
颓陵坏殿名王迹，高塔丛祠旧道场。
泰摆江[1]中楼上月，英雄照尽几沧桑。

罗马京
Rome

1 泰摆江，今译作“台伯河”。罗马建于台伯河之间的七座山岗上。

Touring Capital of Rome and seeing dilapidated two-thousand-year-old cathedrals and palaces all over the place.

Built on and around seven green hills,
A place most calamity stricken among
mountains and rivers on earth.
Hundred-miles of stone channels reaching to a
distant horizon,
Thousand-years old roads dimmed in the
setting sun.
Dilapidated cathedrals, rundown palaces,
all historical sites,
Tall temples, deity shrines, old grounds of rites.
Moon shining over the tower on bank of River Tiber,
Changing times testified well by heroes in history.

罗马有感

坏殿崇楼倚夕阳，教宗霸业两张皇。

东穷舍卫[1]西罗马，大地山河最黯伤。

A Few Thoughts on Rome

Decaying palaces and lofty architectures leaning in sunset,
Both the Pope and autocrats thrown off the edge.
Shevik ruined in the east and Rome ruined in the west,
Vast mountains and rivers fell into hopeless strait.

1 舍卫（Shevik）：位于印度中部的古城，现在的德里。

访四霸遗迹四首

游恺撒[1]故宅，古陵墓通十余里，此葬罗马名人者。断碑碎像，古石数千，购数十事，及初通中国之安敦[2]像归。罗马物入中国自此始。

Around Caesar's former residence, an ancient mausoleum spans over ten miles. Buried here were dignitaries and the upper-crust. Broken tombstones as well as statues, thousand of prehistoric stones scattered around. Made a purchase of some white marble items, including a statue of Emperor Antonius[3], who was the one initiating a relationship with China. Ever since then things from Rome started arriving in China.

---

1 恺撒（Caesar），罗马帝国的奠定者。

2 安敦，即安敦尼王朝五贤帝之安敦尼（138—161 在位），《后汉书》记载其曾派使者来东汉。

3 During the time he was on the throne, Emperor Antonius started a relationship with China by sending diplomatic representatives there, which was recorded in *History of the Late Han Dynasty*.

其一

恺撒生时宅，红墙倚夕阳。

金灯照陵墓，玉匣卧丛冈。

断碣英雄迹，零砖蔓草旁。

搜罗千载物，望古集凄凉。

The former residence of Caesar,
Red walls gleaming in twilight.
Gold lights lit the mausoleum,
Ornamented caskets lay in crest of hills.
Broken stone tablets retaining traces of heroes,
Fragmented bricks among creeping weeds.
In search of thousand-year ancient objects,
A sight of this mess arousing a sense of sadness.

罗马凄凉古迹

Historical Site of Rome

其二

游奥古斯敦[1]遗殿，椒房丹壁，后室无恙，壁画潇洒，似吾江浙派。所遗瓦缶，丹泽盎然。

奥古斯敦殿，遗缶色盎然。
丹青犹在壁，瓦砾几何年。
罗马今为律，飞龙昔在天。
秦皇[2]与汉武，相望孰为贤。

1　奥古斯敦，即罗马第一任皇帝屋大维·奥古斯都。

2　秦皇：中国历史上称古罗马为“大秦”，这里的秦皇指的是罗马安敦朝代皇帝 Antonius Pius 在位（138—161）时。这里，康有为将安敦与汉武帝（前 158—前 87）对比，但是将公元前和公元后搞混了。

In the old palace of Augustin, the empress' private chambers and back rooms were well-preserved. Mural painting elegant and unrestrained in a fashion close to my homeland paintings in Zhejiang style. Pottery lustrous and glossy as ever.

Inside the palace of Augustus[1],
The pottery gleaming in sheen.
Colorfulness still fresh in paintings on the walls,
Alas, from which year were the rubbles formed?
Rome today, a mocked target in the world,
Yet a dragon flying in the sky yesterday.
Roman Empire and Emperor Hanwu[2],
Between them, no one with no errs like saints.

---

1 Augustus (also known as Octavian) was the first emperor of ancient Rome, considered as Father of Rome.

2 Chinese history called Roman Empire "Da Qin", and Emperor Hanwu Dynasty in the first century of Chinese history.

其三

大秦始通中国之主为安敦，守文之贤主也。《后汉书》称其献狮子、符拔，实为欧人交通之始。购其石像归，以纪交通。

狮子兼符拔，通来自大秦。
交通从后汉[1]，第一是安敦。
文化开瀛海，承平创善邻。
我携遗石像，禹域几由旬[2]。

1 后汉，中国朝代名，东汉的别名。

2 由旬（梵 yojana），古印度计程单位。一由旬的长度，我国古有八十里、六十里、四十里等诸说。

The first foreign emperor starting a relationship with China in Qin Dynasty was Antonius Pius, a law-abiding wise ruler at the time. There was a record in *Book of Later Han Dynasty* about him sending China stone lions, talismans, and amulets as presents, which marked the beginning of direct contact between the two countries. I bought a bust of him in memory of his diplomatic mission to China.

Stone lions as well as amulets of different shapes,
All came from the time of Roman Empire.
The first emperor to initiate a diplomatic relationship during Hou Han[1],
Was Emperor Antonius.
Cultures exchanging in the boundless sea,
Flows of trade establishing friendship and peace.
Carrying a bust of Emperor Antonius in my arms,
Without an idea how to reach my own country.

---

1 Hou Han, the Eastern Han Dynasty.

其四

君士但丁[1]有遗殿，户牖尚存，屹然高十丈，其制摩色金盘甚丽，多其遗制，吾曾购得之。

君士但丁帝，雄姿不可方。
丹青[2]有遗殿，户牖半颓墙。
三国归灵统，东都辟裔皇。
金盘摩色[3]丽，娑抚起苍凉。

1 君士坦丁一世于324年重新统一罗马帝国。他是第一位皈依基督教的皇帝，有意把罗马帝国变成一个基督教国家。

2 丹青：绘画，壁画。

3 摩色：即马赛克镶嵌画。

The palace of Constantine I[1], its architecture structure remained intact, towering about ten *zhang* tall, its golden mosaic fronts still magnificent. I purchased a few items from a large collection of relics.

Emperor Constantine I,
His appearance majestic and superb.
Gorgeous paintings remaining in his palace,
Doors and windows hanging on capsizing walls.
Rome's Three-Kingdom Era ended,
With east Byzantine Empire prevailing.
Stroking the golden mosaic front,
A chill started in heart.

1 Constantine I reunified Rome in the 4th century. He was the first Christian emperor and saw the empire begin to become a Christian state.

君士坦丁帝

Emperor Constantine I

古物五章

其一

印埃雅典多遗迹，瑰构雄奇尽石工。

行遍地球看古物，尚看罗马四三雄。

From India, Egypt and Athens,
Stone antiques abundant,
exquisitely unique in shapes.
Traveling around the world to see the antiques,
Objects from Roman period of Triumvirate and
Tetrarch most worth seeing.

其二

颓垣断础二千年，衢道相望自岿然。

最异频缠兵燹乱，保存古物至今传。

Collapsed walls and capsizing corners two-thousand-year old,
In a lofty look, branching roads gazing at each other.
How antiques could survive the ravages of war,
And be preserved so well to this day.

其三

后汉世称风俗美，贼畏明贤鬼读书。
罗马人能存古物，此风粹美又何如。

Hou Han has been known for its fine customs,
Thief feared wise man and book reading a
prevailing trend.
Romans were good at preserving antiques,
A laudable custom indeed.

其四

古物存，可令国增文明。

古物存，可知民敬贤英。

古物存，能令民心感兴。

吁嗟！印度、埃、雅、罗之能存古物兮，

中国乃扫荡而尽平。

甚哉！吾民负文化之名。

With antiques well preserved,
the country's civilization bloomed.
With antiques well preserved,
people's respect for heroes endured.
With antiques well preserved,
people's hearts elevated.
Alas, countries like India, Egypt, Athens, Rome,
All can safeguard ancient objects,
While in China,
antiques dumped and abandoned like trash.
Woe to my people disregarding culture in such
a deplorable way!

其五

埃及陵庙何嵯峨，印度殿塔岁月多。

雅典古庙可婆娑，罗马坏殿遗渠侵云过。

是皆周汉以前物，英雄遗迹啸以歌。

回顾中华无可摩，文明证据空山河。

我心怦怦手自搓，惟有石鼓长城奈若何！

Egypt shrines tall and cragged,
Indian towers century old.
Athens's temples circled around by whirling leaves,
Rome capsized palaces, abandoned channels
wrapped in passing clouds.
Looking back at China, little could be compared,
Ancestral facts before Zhou and Han Dynasties
nowhere to be found.
Mountains and rivers offering no evidences,
Vestiges of heroes only kept in songs.
My heart throbbing and my hands rubbing,
Shame on China that only stone drums and
Great Wall to be proud of!

游邦堆瑜庙[1]

此庙在周与孟子同时，完好可惊，中置意之始王伊曼奴核第一[2]，及画者拉飞尔[3]棺。

邦堆瑜庙二千年，画者名王棺并肩。

叹甚意人尊艺术，此风中土甚惭焉。

1 邦堆瑜庙，即 Pantheon，万神庙。于公元前 27 年兴建，因火灾摧毁，于公元 120 年重建。万神殿 Pantheon 的 pan 是指全部，theon 是神的意思，指必须供奉罗马全部的神。

2 伊曼奴核第一，意大利统一后的第一个国王维克托·伊曼纽尔二世。

3 即意大利画家拉斐尔。

Had a Tour in Pantheon

Built in ancient Mencius era in Zhou Dynasty, its well-preserved beauty struck me greatly. It was the burial place of Victor Emmanuel II, and artist Raphael.

The Pantheon,
a former temple two thousand years of age,
The coffin of the artist and that of the emperor placed side by side.
Marveling at Roman's high respects to arts,
Such a culture put China to a shame.

拉斐尔名画《嘉拉提亚的凯旋》
“Triumph of Galatea” by Raphael

拉斐尔・桑西 (1483—1520)，常称为拉斐尔，意大利著名画家。其作品代表了文艺复兴时期绘画巅峰。

Raffaello Sanzio (1483–1520) was an Italian painter and architect of the High Renaissance. His work is admired for its clarity of form, ease of composition, and visual achievement of the Neoplatonic ideal of human grandeur.

怀意大利拉飞尔画师得绝句八（节选六首）

画师吾爱拉飞尔，创写阴阳妙逼真。
色外生香绕隐秀，意中飞动更如神。

拉君神采秀无伦，生依罗马傍湖滨。
江山秀绝霸图远，妙画方能产此人。

生死婚姻居室处，画图实景尽游之。
弟妹子妻皆写像，同垂不朽画神奇。

拉飞尔画欧人重，一画于今百万金。
我已尽观千百幅，灵光惝恍醉于心。

拉飞尔画多在意，意境以外不可觅。
只有巴黎数幅存，瑰宝珍于连城璧。

拉飞尔画非人力，秀韵神光属化工。
太白[1]诗词右军[2]字，天然清水出芙蓉。

---

1 太白，中国古代诗人李白。

2 右军，王羲之(303—361)，中国古代书法家。

A Poem on Praising Italian Artist Raphael (6 Excerpts)

My favorite artist Raphael,
His art mastery excelling in versatility.
Featuring delicacy, clarity, and rich color,
Achieving visual clarity of human grandeur.

Raphael's appearance most handsome and graceful,
Born in a lakeside city in Rome,
growing to be a great artist.
Splendid paints created,
So a superb artist emerged.

He drew about life, death, marriage,
All human life truthfully portrayed.
His renderings of human form:
men, women, children,
All with exceptional grace and an enduring beauty.

Raphael's paintings were mostly European figures,
One painting was worth of a million dollars.
Although I have seen hundreds of them,

My heart still drunk in their stunning beauty.

Raphael's paintings had been kept strictly in Italy,
Hardly any painting could be found outside Italy.
Only Paris had a display of a few,
Priceless treasures cherished more than
valuable gems.

Raphael's paintings seemed not from a human hand,
But artful pieces of celestial work from heaven.
Like Taibai's poetry, Youjun's calligraphy[1],
Fresh and distinguished lotus rising out of
clear water.

1 Taibai, Chinese ancient poet; Youjun, Chinese ancient calligrapher.

1904 年 6 月 23 日，游拜西诃公园[1]，适遇某诗人立像揭幕，旌旗车马，士女如云。

公园十里拜西诃，士女如云警吏呵。
万众免冠旗影绕，诗人[2]立像敬恭多。

On June 23, 1904, Kang Youwei toured in Villa Borghese, a park situated in Pincio. There he witnessed the opening ceremony of the monument to the great German writer Johann Wolfgang von Goethe (1749–1832). The monument was a present from Germany to Rome as a sign of the friendship between the Italians and Germans and in memory of the hospitality the city of Pincio towards the poet Goethe when he lived there.

1 拜西诃公园，即 Pincio Park，今译作“品奇欧”，是意大利重要的社交活动场所。

2 诗人，即德国诗人歌德（康有为没有认出雕像是谁，是因为晚上导游下班了，他们自由行，所以不知道）。

The park in Pincio ten miles vast,
Banners waving and flags fluttering.
A huge throng of men and women,
As well as policemen keeping order.
All hats-off and in full respect,
On this ceremonial inauguration of the
monument to a poet[1].

德国诗人歌德塑像，罗马拜西诃公园
German Writer Johann Wolfgang Von Goethe, Pincio Park, Rome

1 Poet refers to German writer Johann Wolfgang von Goethe (Kang didn't recognize him).

期间康有为还参观了许多基督教教堂。

During the days in Rome, Kang Youwei also visited many churches.

罗马四百寺，道中及公园，极目皆僧。

缁徒[1]市里道相望，遗室参经古道场。

罗马名蓝四百寺，几多塔殿对斜阳。

There were four hundred churches in Rome. In the streets or in the parks, clergymen could be seen all the time.

Clergymen, a frequent sight in the streets,
Abandoned shrines often meeting ritual grounds.
Rome had four hundred principal churches,
Tops and towers glowing in the slanting sun.

1 缁徒：僧侣。

自罗马北行至瑞士道中。

冈峦四绵亘，果树剪平齐。

山颠抗楼阁，郊外尽菩提。

野女红兼白，山田高及低。

夕来明月大，逐我汽车西。

On the road from Rome to Switzerland.

Rolling hills stretching in unbroken chain,
Fruit treetops trimmed nicely even.
Houses standing on top of the hills,
Banyan trees seen everywhere in the country.
Girls in red and white busy in the fields,
Hillside plots lining from high to low.
Night fell, bringing out a moon big and bright,
Chasing after our train west bound.

维苏威火山[1]
Mount Vesuvius 1904

从被摧毁的庞贝视角观维苏威火山

Mount Vesuvius Seen from Ruins of Pompeii

1 维苏威火山是一座活火山，位于意大利南部那不勒斯湾东海岸，是世界最著名的火山之一，被誉为“欧洲最危险的火山”。

观斐苏斐（今译作“维苏威”）火山，返及山麓，倚酒楼望海，并眺奈波里全城，华人莫我先也。

晨登斐苏斐，中午饭山麓。
酒楼凭高处，开窗纵游目。
海山两门峙，海波浩荡绿。
岛屿荡烟点，帆樯渺相属。
楼阁抗丘陵，临海环华屋。
波涛拍石岸，风起奏笙筑。
人家六十万，烟树弥望缛。
葡萄梅杏李，累累枝头熟。
都会二千年，英雄战争酷。
德法与奥班，争霸来逐鹿。
近起烧炭党[1]，竟成统一局。
虽历火山灾，岂舍胜地曲。
山海控要妙，阛阓伟瞻瞩。

1 烧炭党，意大利资产阶级的秘密革命团体，成立于十九世纪初，因成员最初逃避在南部 烧炭山区而得名。

吾华与相比，芝罘[1]犹少缩。
大风波忽荡，炎日正当旭。
长啸眺大宇，天海在一掬。
引杯且陶然，旅人登快足。
支那来游者，吾先谁为续。

Today, having visited Mount Vesuvius, I returned to the foot of the mountain where my hotel was. From the hotel, I had a full view of the sea as well as the whole city of Napoli. No Chinese tourist had ever been here before me.

Climbed Mount Vesuvius in the morning,
And returned to the mountain base for lunch at noon.
The hotel towering on high,
Its windows opening a sweeping view.
Beyond the sea, two mountains gazing at each other,
Sea waves forming a vast expanse of green.
Smoky islets dotting the sea,
Ship masts and spars packed close in water.

1 芝罘，即今日之山东烟台。

Pavilions adorning the hills,
Elegant government buildings encircling the sea.
Constant sea waves lapping stone shores,
Wind playing pleasant music.
Six hundred thousand households,
an eye-full view of wonders,
Grapes, plums, apricots,
fruits heavy and ripe on the trees.
A metropolis for two thousand years,
Undergoing wars with Germany, France,
Hungary, Spain,
Each greedy, scrambling here, striving for hegemony.
Owing to Carbonari's[1] role,
An independent unified country was born.
Although devastated several times by volcanic eruptions,
The land's highlights and historic interests
luckily unscathed.
Napoli's geological advantage sustained the city,
Its cityscape remained a gorgeous sight.
In comparison with my China's Cheefo[2],
It's smaller in size.
Here, gusts of strong wind ruffling the sea,

---

1 Carbonari, asecret revolutionary organization founded in the early 19th century that played an important role in the unification of Italy.

2 Cheefo, a city in Shandong Province, well-known for its nice cityscape.

Noon's sunshine bright and direct.
Uttering a shout,
The sky and sea between my fingers.
Holding a cup in ecstasy,
I am an early pilgrim.
A tourist from China like me,
Who will be the next?

加拿大
Canada 1899–1904

地中海
Mediterranean 1904

意大利
Italy 1904

瑞士
Switzerland 1904

法国
France 1904

1904 年 6 月 26 日，康有为从罗马北上，穿过阿尔卑斯山脉来到瑞士城市卢塞恩，初到瑞士。1906 年 8 月再次过瑞士，居柳街诺，作诗。瑞士国在阿尔频山[1]中，湖山之胜，游客之盛，为天下第一，吾两过之，后遂五游[2]。

On August 1906, Kang Youwei went northbound from Roman, crossed the Alps and arrived at Lucerne, Switzerland. Switzerland located in the Alps, is number one for its beauty of mountains and lakes, as well as abundant tourists. I have been to Lucerne twice. Also I went to Lugano in August 1906, then visited capital Bern, Geneva and Zurich. So I called it my Five Trips to Switzerland.

---

1 阿尔频山，今译作“阿尔卑斯山”。

2 1907 年 11 月又到瑞士首都伯尔尼，尔后又陆续经过瑞士日内瓦和苏黎世，故曰五游。

瑞士非国土，乃是大公园。苍苍阿尔频，岳镇中欧尊。陂沱溃下南北海，欧洲百国皆仆缘。瑞士千里何盘盘，山中辟国五百年。南朝罗马、北通德志必经焉。

昔者封建战焚煎，山民自保障垒坚。
七十邑部盟密联，北与汉堡市府相应牵。
奥霸轻视等羌蛮，频遣轻兵败不前。
新旧教争大鏖搏，遂令自立开桃源。
太平共和廿二村，无君无臣乐便便。
葡萄连架农之田，时表精妙良工传。
花牛漫山鱼满川，以牧以渔时狩畋。
雪色皑皑照青天，碧松遍山草芊芊。
碧绿丘壑白峰峦，山巅成千湖，明漪动紫澜。
小湖柳攲[1]波，荡桨烧风烟。
大湖数百里，诸峰浸其间。
虹桥苔矶间绿阑，万千楼阁枕湖干。

1 “攲”是依靠的意思，但是攲常会与水波连用，古文又作“倚”，所以选“攲”。

抗山架壑高下繁，白塔红亭冠山巅。
水榭林屋隐涧泉，汽船翻浪穿湖边。
铁轨穴隧上山巅，欧洲诸国程途便。
一日二日至翩翩，帝王妃主微行先。
将相公侯贵王孙，骚人名士揄袂联。
大贾富商随喜迁，相将蜡屐赋游仙。
别墅行宫望离离，旌旗飞扬压翠微。
客舍华严百亿扉，沿崖夹涧随日移。
仕女霓裳曳羽衣，盛夏清凉相携嬉。
水滨草际行卧宜，听瀑登山泛湖湄。
幔亭茶舫泊无时，球场猎犬无绊羁[1]。
夕归观剧浴香霏，南柳街诸北垆顺。
临湖佳胜天所资，冬时避寒客筛离。
万峰雪色尤离披，寸岑尺土绿玻璃。
乐国乐土无复之，我两过此罄其奇。
胜地胜游古今稀，梦回天际之峰莽不离[2]。

1　绊羁，意思为羁绊。

2　莽不离（Mont Blanc），即勃朗峰，阿尔频山绝顶。

Switzerland rather like an enormous park than just being land of a country. The majesty of the Alps topping all the mountains in Europe. From mountain slopes, torrential water rushing down into the South and North seas, flowing past and building bonds with a hundred of European countries. The highest and most extensive Alps ranges, covering most of Switzerland for five hundred years. Stretching thousands of miles across Rome in the south and Germany in the north.

Enduring years of suffering from feudal wars,
Mountain villagers built fortifications protecting their homes.
Seventy cities of the country closely knit together,
Its north border connecting with Germany's Hamburg.
Aggressive Austrians misjudging southerner Swiss' ability,
Frequent military menaces ending only in self-defeat.
Long lasting game of Old and New Religions,
Religious autonomy prompting peach blossoms in the land.
Establishment of peace and republicanism in

twenty two communities,
A state with no monarchical authority making people happy.
Clusters of grape hanging full on trellis,
easy farming in fertile field,
Watch-making famous for expert precision and unparalleled craftsmanship.
Mountains full of black and white cattle,
lakes full of assorted fish,
Making a living by grazing,
fishing and hunting sometimes.
White snow gleaming on mountain summits under blue sky,
Pine trees covering mountains,
a full view of lush green.
Emerald hills and ravines surrounded by white ridges and peaks,
Mountaintops overlooking thousands of lakes.
Clear water rippling purple waves,
Paddling a boat and rowing it with misty wind.
Large lakes extending hundred of miles,
Mountains standing within lake,
peeping heads out of water.
Under the rainbow bridges,
green water flowing between the mossy rocks,

Thousands of houses surrounding the lakes.
Mountain climbing every day's tough expedition,
White towers and red pavilions crowning the tops.
Houses hidden amidst mountain springs,
Piercing waves, steamboats dashing past lakeside.
Railways circling through tunnels up to
mountaintops,
Easiest transportation among European countries.
Taking one day or two to reach Switzerland,
Kings and queens arriving first.
Followed by generals and noblemen,
As well as celebrities and wealthy businessmen.
Villas and palaces waiting on distant mountains,
Colorful banners fluttering, muffling green scenery.
Extravagant hotels with millions of windows,
Alongside the cliffs streams of water trickling down.
Graceful ladies in elegant feather-light attire,
Playing joufully in cool summer air.
Lying on waterside grass a relaxing pastime,
Listening to waterfall, mountain climbing,
and riding a boat.
Sitting idle over tea in pavilions as long as you like,
Pet dogs free to run about without restrictions.
Returning in the sunset,
watching a play then taking a fragrant bath,

Either staying in south Lugano or staying in north Luzern.
Both superb lakeside resorts under God,
Staying in warm Zurich in cold winter season.
Snow-capped mountaintops,
coupled with fresh green meadows,
A magnificent sight to behold.
Happy country, happy land, not a comparable place in the whole world,
Lucky me to have traveled here two times.
Rare sightseeing opportunity of scenic beauty Switzerland,
Returning to my dream will be Mont Blanc touching sky!

瑞士勃朗峰 Mont Blanc, Switzerland

瑞士
Switzerland 1904

法国
France 1904

德国
Germany 1904

奥地利
Austria 1904

匈牙利
Hungary 1904

1904年7月5日，康有为参观完德国埃森（Essen）市的军工巨头克虏伯兵工厂后，前往法国。在法国博物馆，康有为发现中国清朝的玉玺，大为伤感。

On July 5, 1904, Kang Youwei visited the military giant Krupp Arsenal in Essen. Then he left Germany, heading for France. In Paris Museum, Kang Youwei spotted royal seals from China's Qing Dynasty, his heart hurt with great pain.

巴黎博物馆
Paris Museum

巴黎睹圆明春山玉玺，思旧游感赋（节选）

宫苑深深老柳卧，荷花开尽无人过。

苇桥渡入福海[1]中，白石台殷倚白松。

白头宫监犹守护，凄然僵柏起长风。

蔓草荒烟堆瓦砾，玲珑白阁犹奕奕。

门户百千尽欧式，圣祖手作着象历。

忆昔霓旌幸苑时，畴人南汤来侍值。

寿山春日饶物华，辇路繁花好颜色。

罗刹远遣图理琛，荷兰贡入量天尺。

当时威廉始入英，人民不及五十亿[2]。

欧土文明未开化，惟我威灵照八极。

百年之间新世变，汽船铁轨通重驿。

惜哉闭关守长夜，竟尔绝海召强敌。

1 福海，北京圆明园内景色优美的福海景区。

2 五十亿，古人称十万为亿，五十亿即现在的五百万。

阿房一炬[1]光亘天，热河[2]三年泪沾臆。
小臣步履伤怀抱，手抚铜驼叹荆棘。
岂意京邑两丘墟[3]，玉玺落此无人识。
雨夜淋铃几度闻，追思故苑满春云。
逋臣万里游巴黎，摩挲遗玺心凄凄。
尚想承平春苑道，千官拥从豹尾麾。
黄屋龙旌绕朝晖，八校无哗万马蹄。

---

1 阿房一炬，本意指阿房宫，诗里意指1860年圆明园被英法联军焚毁。

2 热河，中国旧行政区划的省份之一，省会承德是清朝皇室的避暑胜地，辛酉政变的发生地。

3 京邑两丘墟，圆明园和故宫。

Summer Palace's Chunshan Royal Seal Found in Paris Museum

Old willow twigs resting in the depth of the palace court,
Lotus blossom long over, nobody noticed.
Bridge in shade of reeds leading to scenic Fuhai[1] lake,
White stone platform against intertwined white pines.
White-headed court eunuchs still guarding at the gate,
Gusts of wind blowing among dead pines.
Weeds creeping over desolate rubble heaps,
Elegant white pavilion still an attractive view.
Architecture styles all European,
Astrological calendars designed by former emperors.
Once flags of colorful feathers filling the court,
Skillful, astronomer from Nantang coming to serve.
Mount Wanshou in spring a beautiful embodiment of nature,

1 Fuhai, a scenic lake in Summer Palace.

Passing carriages adorned with colorful flowers.
Russia sent out spies afar,
Dutch sent an altimeter as tribute.
When William I first came to be king in Britain,
It's a country with population less than five million[1].
European civilization then not yet developed,
While my country's almighty already shinning
over octapole.
In less than a century, alas, things all turned around,
Steamships, railways reaching main cities everywhere.
Woe to China's long term closed-door policy,
Powerful foes looming large from the sea.
Efang Palace[2] set afire,
The sky ablaze with flames.
Royal family taking refuge in Jehol[3] for three years,
Thinking of this, tears came quickly wetting clothes.
Staggering along, my heart drowning with sorrow,
By scene of devastation of the burned-down palace.

---

1 Ancient Chinese called 100,000 a billion.

2 Efang Palace set afire, It refers to the burning of the Old Summer Palace by Anglo-French forces in 1860.

3 Jehol, an old Province, in its capital Chengde was a summer resort for the Royal family of Qing Dynasty. When the Anglo-French forces captured Beijing, the Qing imperial family took refuge in Jehol for three years (1860-1862).

Two great palaces[1] should have been destroyed
at the same time,
No one knew how royal seals found their way
to Paris.
Night rain striking doorbells keeping me awake,
A heart lost in fond memory of the old palace in spring.
I came to Paris from thousands of miles away,
Remembering the royal seal,
my heart gripped in pain.
Imagining peace and order returning to the
capital in spring,
A large retinue marching,
leopard tail banners fluttering.
Clip-clop of hooves of a thousand horses resounding,
Dragon flags on yellow palace glowing in
sunlit morning.

1 Referring to the Old Summer Palace and the Imperial Palace.

圆明园于 1860 年 10 月 18 日被英法联军焚烧

The Old Summer Palace Burned Down on October 18, 1860 by Anglo-French Forces

懋勤殿玉玺

忆昨维新变法时，延英选士赞黄扉。
明堂大启咨群议，草泽旁求助万机。
岂料群龙成血战，当年二凤[1]话齐飞。
凄凉回首懋勤殿，玉玺迁流国事非。

懋勤殿

碧玉玺
长方寸半
篆　文

懋勤殿玉玺
Maoqin Hall Royal Seal

1　二凤，指咸丰八年（1858）何秋涛和郭嵩焘两位通达时务，晓畅戎机，被称为“双凤齐飞”。

Maoqin Hall Royal Seal

Recalling yesterday's Reform Movement,
Best elites being chosen in yellow royal building.
Palace hall opened for government consultation,
Beneficial opinions from common heads heard and considered.

Who would foresee a host of dragons coming to bloody blows?
Parted were the two phoenixes[1] once flying in good harmony.
Looking back sadly at the Hall of Heavenly Purity,
The royal seal belonging to the palace gone and state of affairs altered.

---

1 Two phoenixes refer to like-minded comrades once working in good harmony.

游花赊喇[1]路易十四宫

阿房三百里，仿佛见秦皇。
迹是瑶台后，花繁上苑旁。
舞鸾犹镜殿，画像遍椒房。
拂拭金人泪，英雄事可伤。
追思繁盛日，宴剧压迷楼。
三千备宫女，十万走诸侯。
歌舞收雄据，貂蝉艳贵游。
隐销封建患，英主自深谋。
欧土千年乱，封侯肇不宁。
兵戈虽满野，磬石结雄城。
封建从销弭，民权乃发生。
夜呼闻涉广，宪法大横庚。

1　花赊喇宫，即凡尔赛宫。

Visiting Palace of Versailles of Louis XIV

Efang palace occupying a land of 300 miles,
Feeling as if Emperor Qin were in his palace.
Exquisite terrace ornate with jade ornaments,
Luxuriant flowers beautifying gardens.
Mythical birds dancing in mirror-reflecting halls,
Portraits and paintings hanging full on palace walls.
Wiping out tears of the little gold Buddha,
Heroic deeds could be sad and hurtful.
Recalling old thriving days,
Banquets and operas, a hilarious labyrinth.
Three thousand palace maids ready to serve,
Plus ten thousand traveling marquises.
Singing and dancing non-stop while territory being divided,
Charming girls entertaining distinguished guests from abroad.
To eliminate perennial hidden danger of feudalism,
Wise kings handling it well with strategies.
European land being war-torn for a thousand years,
Appointing high official posts only causing strife.
Troops carried off all over the battlefield,
Rocky siege ramps breaching fortified city.

Feudalism finally put to an end,
Democracy and civil rights coming into practice.
I, well informed from all the news,
Knowing constitutions being spread across
global landscape.

圆明园宫殿残骸

Burned-down Palace in the Old Summer Palace

在法国南部，除了葡萄酒和歌剧外，康有为对这里房屋、道路等民生建设不很满意。

Kang Youwei thought that there was nothing good in the south of France, except wine and opera. There the houses, roads and infrastructure were all outdated.

自法之南行六解 1907年1月

法国唯巴黎胜妙，法南贫秽，不足观也。

自法之南，草泽沮洳。
平冈大原，千里土腴。
何以种之，青青葡萄。
自法之南，屋矮地污。
墙或及肩，贫多役夫。
草具牛衣，马牛其躯。
自法之南，行彼旷野。
役夫筑墙，言逢零雨。
张盖吸烟，卧于堤下。

自法之南，奸与尼士[1]。
依山临海，风景美处。
楼阁华妙，避寒多住。
自法之南，言过波多[2]。
表海大都，霸业消磨。
旧坏泥污，不治则那。
惟多美酒，听剧且歌。
自法之南，三至马赛[3]。
海山幽绿，都市矜夸。
登塔天宇，走马海涯。
不寒不碧，山曲可家。

1 奸与尼士，即戛纳与尼斯。

2 即波尔多（Bordeaux），法国西南部城市。

3 马赛（Marseille）是法国第三大城市。康有为此行三过马赛。

Going Down South in France

Apart from fancy Paris, places in France especially the southern part of France were unworthy of seeing at all.

Going down south in France,
Swampy and damp.
Vast stretches of flat plains,
Thousands of miles of fertile land.
What had been grown there?
Green grapes only.

Going down south in France,
Houses low and landscape filthy.
Walls about shoulder's height,
Laborers not wealthy.
Herding cattle and feeding horses,
Driving cattle and horses side by side.

Going down south in France,
Wilderness areas often to be crossed.
Servants putting up enclosures,
Quite often exposed to rain.
Sticking head out for cigarette smoking,
Lying down with back against embankment.

Going down south in France,
Visiting seaside cities Cannes and Nice.
Surrounded by mountains facing the sea,
Scenic beauty marvelous.
Temples and pavilions, graceful and stylish,
Nice places to stay as resort for winter.

Going down south in France,
Arriving at Bordeaux,
A coastal city,
Its dominant business declining.
Decaying infrastructure,
Uncared-for and letting it go.
Choicest wine abundant and,
Operas fancy watching and hearing.

Going down south in France,
Three times stopped at Marseilles.
A green sight of mountains and sea,
A metropolitan boastful of its fine being.
Climbing up towers to touch the sky,
Riding a horse along the seaside.
A place not remote nor cold,
A place suitable for comfortable living indeed.

瑞士
Switzerland 1904

法国
France 1904

德国
Germany 1904

奥地利
Austria 1904

匈牙利
Hungary 1904

1904 年 6 月 30 日，康有为从瑞士前往奥匈帝国途中经过巴伐利亚[1]首府慕尼黑。

欧美道路之洁，以德联邦湃认[2]国免恨京为第一。公园依山，溪流穿郭，楼阁明靓，亦冠全欧也。

On June 30, 1904, Kang Youwei went from Switzerland to the Austro-Hungarian Empire via Bavaria[3] capital Munich.

Streets in Bayern were number-one for their clean and neat look. Situated near a river and a mountain, its park ranked among one of the best in Europe with its clean stream waters and gorgeous temples and pavilions.

---

1 巴伐利亚（Bavaria），位于德国南部，昔时为一独立王国。

2 湃认，即拜仁，德意志联邦共和国东南部一州，昔属巴伐利亚，今即慕尼黑。

3 Bavaria, located at South Germany and was an independent kingdom in the old days.

免恨[1]京三咏

其一

白道光华免恨京，楼台新靓照人明。

万绿压园倚丘壑，六衢绕水听波声。

Clean and neat streets in Munich,

Gorgeous new temples, an eye pleasing view.

With a hill at the back,

Flourishing foliage painting the park green.

Stream water surrounding six roads,

Uttering sound soothing and pleasant.

十九世纪的昔属巴伐利亚，即今慕尼黑

Munich, Bavaria in 19th Century

1 免恨，以及下文的冕痕，皆指慕尼黑(Munich)。

其二

啤酒尤传免恨名，创于湃认路易倾。

吾曾人饮王酒店，三千人醉饮如鲸。

啤酒创于湃认王路易，德音呼王为倾。（吾性不饮酒，德食店不饮者多出一擘。）有王酒店，吾饮焉，大容三千人，沉湎常满饮者，琉璃杯大如斗。然德人之肥泽，由啤酒醉不害事，亦饮中之佳品也。

Most popular beer was from Munich,
Brewery founded by the Duke of Bavaria.
I went to the oldest beer hall to try the beer,
Amazed to see three thousand people binge drinking like whale.
Original recipes handed down from the Duke of Bavaria, Beer named The Hof[1] coming from the royal brewery in the Kingdom of Bavaria.
The beer hall also a royal property,

1 Hof (Hofbräuhaus) is the oldest beer brand in Germany.

Able to hold as many people as three thousand.
I tasted beer there,
Immersed in hilarious people drinking from mugs the size of a bucket.
Germany, most brawny and overweight,

Having nothing to do with their beer drinking,
Beer is the best of beverages indeed.

Beer was created by Lord Louis of Bavaria, and German called Lord as King. I used not to drink, as the restaurant would charge 10% extra if a person drank no beer. I tried beer at Kings Brewery, where it could hold about 3,000 people and was often full, people drank beer with mugs as big as buckets. Germans were mostly big, yet their obesity had little to do with their beer drinking. Beer was a quite healthy beverage.

啤酒厂 The Former Hofbräuhaus

啤酒厅 Inside Hofbräuhaus Beer Hall

Drinking Beer In Munich

Most popular beer was from Munich,
Brewery founded by the Duke of Bavaria.
I went to the oldest beer hall to try the beer,
Amazed to see three thousand people binge drinking like whale.
Original recipes handed down from the Duke of Bavaria,
Beer named The Hof[1] coming from the royal brewery in the Kingdom of Bavaria.
The beer hall also a royal property,
Able to hold as many people as three thousand.
I tasted beer there,
Immersed in hilarious people drinking from mugs the size of a bucket.
Germany, most brawny and overweight,
Having nothing to do with their beer drinking,
Beer is the best of beverages indeed.

1 Hof (Hofbräuhaus) is the oldest beer brand in Germany.

此外，在慕尼黑公园里，康有为看见了孔子和老子的画像，这让他惊奇不已。"公园画楼正楼，陈十余前哲像，孔子老子二像列焉，全欧只见此耳。"

In that park, Kang Youwei saw portraits of Confucius and Laozi which surprised him greatly. "At the front of the art gallery in the park, ten portraits or so were in display, among which were portraits of Confucius and Laozi."

欧人论学东哲轻，德人好学康德[1]唱。
免恨公园画院中，独见庄严孔老像。

Europeans' preference of philosophy study,
Valuing the west over the east,
German thought Immanuel Kant[2] most important.
Yet in the gallery of the park,
Only solemn portraits of Confucius and Laozi[3]
to be seen.
These two portraits in display,
Impossible to be found elsewhere in whole Europe.

1 康德（1724—1805），德国哲学家，古典唯心主义的创始人。

2 Kant (1724—1805), German philosopher, the founder of classical idealist philosophy.

3 Confucius and Laozi, ancient Chinese philosophers.

游柏林诗（节选于《游柏林议院诗》）

我来游柏林，道路广以净。

植树列四行，行人想以咏。

汉堡与冕痕，周道如砥镜。

万国治道路，无如德光莹。

士女畏游徼[1]，子夜百戏静。

政治既严肃，文学复明盛。

1 游徼，即巡逻警察 (patrolling police)。

Poem on Berlin

(Extract from Poem "Touring Berlin Congress Building")

I came to visit Berlin,
Its streets broad and clean.
Trees planted in four rows,
Pedestrians so pleased with the scene.
Hamburg as well as Munich,
Streets were like grinding stones.
Road condition compared with other nations,
Few had such shining merits.
Here men and women had a fear of patrolling police,
Midnight fell into total silence.
Politics a serious matter,
Literature and art buzzing and revitalized.

柏林观剧，有十三岁女儿入狮槛抚狮，骑之，抱之，鞭之，同卧，以首入狮口，皆可神乎技矣。

弄狮女儿亦神全，绿衣入槛抱狮眠。
起执长鞭骑狮走，不畏狮吼如普贤。

I watched a circus lion performance in Berlin: Entering the ring was a girl only thirteen, she caressed the lion, rode on it, held it, whipped it, and laid down beside it, and even put her head into its mouth. Her performing acts all terrific!

The lion-playing girl was awe-inspiring and amazing.
In green costume she got into the ring,
And patted the lion down to sleep.
Standing up, she rode on it, a lash in hand,
Fearless of lion's roaring like a wise woman.

游普鲁士[1]旧京波士淡[2]之阿朗赊理宫[3]，睹宫前陈元郭太史[4]所制浑天仪、黄、赤道及象限仪五器。诸仪器前摩挲于京师观象台者也，二十余年重逢异域，感怀身世，悲从中来，不觉涕之被面也。作长诗一首，铭记国耻。

陂陀葱郁普旧京，诃厘湖[5]波一碧平。
离宫别馆三十六，掩映林麓见飞惊。
苹果屈篱兽喷水，数里幽绿围青城。
崇冈危级花畦绣，上据殿阁何峥嵘。
长方楼塔横百丈，扣墀文石登三成。
草间花际徘徊步，忽睹宝器心怦怦。
紫铜圆球大盈丈，周围刻缀皆天星。
太微紫薇横天市，二十八宿何荧荧。
以手摩挲重叹惜，泪痕盈面涕沾臆。
吁嗟此为浑天仪，太史以制授时历。
作者元初郭守敬，独明绝学任天官。

1　普鲁士（Prussia），主要位于现在的德国。
2　波士淡，即德国波茨坦（Potsdam）。
3　阿朗赊理宫，即橘园宫（Orangery Palace）。
4　陈元郭太史，郭守敬，中国元朝大科学家，编制《授时历》，任知太史院事。
5　诃厘湖（Heiliger See），今译“海利格湖”或“圣湖”。

光绪八年秋七月，吾游京师来橐笔。
生平颇好天文学，登台摩挲细考析。
岂意别后廿余载，波士淡京重遭值。
同是华京沦落客，相逢相吊感畴昔。
绝域隔海三万里，问君无足无羽翼。
何能飞来德意志，载以巨舶裹以席。
从来瑰宝非一国，多难遘遭劫千亿。
国土文明寄重器，何图天球逾拱璧。
文献遗留吾与汝，身世飘零多感激。
鸟啼花落此何地，白发重摩伤逋客。
异时若登观象台，呼天难问云惨碧。

中国古代浑天仪
Chinese armillary sphere

Visiting the Orangery Palace in Potsdam, Germany, Kang Youwei spotted an armillary sphere, a sextant etc. five astronomical instruments that were made by Guo Shoujing[1] of the Yuan Dynasty. He clearly remembered the time he touched and stroked those instruments when visiting Beijing Ancient Observatory more than twenty years ago. In agony, and with tears filling eyes, Kang wrote a long poem to remember this national shame.

Lush landscape extends out over hilly Prussia,
Heiliger See a smooth stretch of green waves.
Leaving the imperial palace,
Walking in mountain thicket,
startled by flying birds passing.
Fruits from apple trees peeping out of fences,
Animal-shaped fountains keeping spitting water.
Miles of thriving foliage encircling the city,
Flowery embroidered ridges mocked by high hills,
On which the arrogant palace boasted its brilliance.
The rectangle palace a hundred *zhang* in width,
A flight of stairs inlaid with gold and jade

1 Guo Shoujing, the greatest scientist of the Yuan Dynasty, who designed Timing Calendar and was appointed to be the Imperial Astronomer.

leading to its entrance.
My steps wandering about on grass charmed with flowers,
My heart still pounding having seen all the treasures.
A red copper ball well over a *zhang* in diameter,
Celestial stars carved full on its surface.
Crape myrtle with supreme subtlety enclose,
Twenty-eight constellations glimmering in silence.
Giving it a gentle caress, heaving a sigh of heartache,
Tears and snot running down,
front of my jacket wet.
My heart in pain for this armillary sphere,
Invented by Guo Shoujing from Yuan Dynasty.
A talented man with unique vision who designed the Timing Calendar,
Appointed to be Imperial Astronomer in the country.
In the fall of 1882, I came to Yanjing[1],
Serving as a counsellor.
Being a lover of astronomy,
I mounted the observatory platform and took a close look of it.
More than twenty years had passed,
Never did I think I would see you again in Potsdam!

---

1 Yanjing: Beijing.

You and me, both drifters from China,
Comforting each other here, regretting the past.
Being far away from a sea of 30,000 *li*,
Neither had you feet or wings.
How did you get to Germany?
Could be wrapped in a mat and carried in a
colossal vessel.
National treasures could not be protected in
the country,
Calamity befell, treasures plundered,
a value of billions of dollars.
A nation's civilization values historical objects,
The celestial sphere went beyond the arch wall.
Historical legacy, both you and me,
Should we be thankful for our drifting life experience?
A desolate sight of birds singing with flowers fading,
My hair's turning gray, my heart going out for you,
A wounded hermit in solitude.
As if mounting onto the observatory platform,
I cry out to heaven, questioning why the clouds
are looking so bleak.

橘园宫坐落在德国波茨坦

The Orangery Palace is located in the Sanssouci Park of Potsdam

瑞士
Switzerland 1904

法国
France 1904

德国
Germany 1904

奥地利
Austria 1904

匈牙利
Hungary 1904

1904年6月29日，康有为离开瑞士卢塞恩，经过瑞士与德国、奥地利交界处的博登湖，借道德国巴伐利亚慕尼黑来到奥匈帝国。随后游览了维也纳，康有为对那里众多的咖啡馆印象深刻。

维也纳的咖啡馆文化被列为非物质世界文化遗产，到了维也纳旅游不去咖啡馆会留下遗憾。

维也纳（Vienna）乃英音，若奥音作湾（德语：Wien），名从主人，后仿此。

On June 29, 1904, Kang Youwei left Lucerne, Switzerland, passing Lake Bodensee (Constance in English) at the junction of Switzerland, Germany and Austria, going through Munich, and finally arrived at Austria. He toured around the capital Vienna, and had a deep impression of its coffee culture.

Vienna is best known for its coffee culture and its cafés have been listed as a World Intangible Cultural Heritage. Therefore, drinking coffee in a Vienna café has been considered a thing in the to-do list for tourists.

The name Vienna's pronunciation is from English, and in Austrian, it is pronounced Wien, whose name was given by its inhabitants.

维也纳咖啡馆 Café in Vienna

湾京咏

湾京旧霸统，气象比巴黎。

宫馆皆崒丽，林途尽广齐。

柏林嗟幼稚，伦敦狭模规。

感慨邯郸市[1]，今朝落泰西[2]。

1 邯郸市，河北省旧时的城市，后失去都市的位置。

2 泰西，旧称西方包括欧美。

A Poem on the Capital Vienna

Capital Vienna, a city boastful of its blend of
artistic and intellectual legacy,
With a charm as endearing as Paris.
Showcasing its gorgeous imperial palaces,
Splendid landmarks everywhere,
As well as its broad and straight streets.
In comparison of its cityscape,
Berlin seems a little immature,
London seems a little too crowded for its size.
Lamenting our Chinese city Handan[1],
Fallen in the hands of the Western colonization.

---

1 Handan, an old city in Hebei Province which had lost its importance with the passing of time.

瑞士
Switzerland 1904

法国
France 1904

德国
Germany 1904

奥地利
Austria 1904

匈牙利
Hungary 1904

游完奥地利都城维也纳的康有为顺道前往匈牙利都城布达佩斯，在那里康有为看了歌剧。（匈牙利标德卑士[1]京甚妙丽，其长堤夹多铙河[2]，电灯铁几，车马如织，士女相携，园林精妙，好乐似巴黎。匈人本游牧，善为乐声，小国僻壤有此，盖欧东阿连[3]五国[4]人所走集也。）

1　标德卑士（Budapest），即布达佩斯。

2　多铙河，即多瑙河。

3　阿拉伯连通处

4　五国，指奥斯曼帝国、罗马尼亚、保加利亚、黑山、塞尔维亚。

After Vienna, Austria, Kang Youwei headed for Hungary's capital Budapest. He watched opera there. Hungary's capital Budapest is a stylish and sophisticated metropolitan. Bisected by the Danube River, the city has its water rolling in between the long embankments of both sides. Highly impressive are its brilliant lights at night, continuous flow of horses and carriages, beautiful landscape with exquisite gardens and parks, and remarkable musicals, each equalling those in Paris. Hungarians used to be nomadic people who were gifted with vocal talent. A small landlocked country situated at the intersection of Ottoman Empire, Hungary has been attracting migrants and tourists from neighboring countries, such as Turkey, Romania, Bulgaria, Montenegro, Serbia and so on.

匈京虽僻小，人号小巴黎。
道路广以洁，楼阁丽欲迷。
滔滔多锐河，花木夹长堤。
铁桥连锁之，山水泻清辉。
明月照裙屐，车马如龙飞。
堤长十馀里，士女相扶携。
议院与王宫，壮丽河东西。
夜游百戏园，灯火亿万枝。
游牧琵琶声，佳人红玉肌。
信哉古郑卫[1]，游乐人不讥。
从今欧土国，后作胜前徽。
逆想后百年，迷楼与天齐。

1 郑卫，指“郑卫之曲”，春秋时期郑国和卫国的民间音乐，出自《史记·乐书》。儒家认为其音淫靡，不同于雅乐，故斥之为淫声，但却是民间喜好的音乐。

Although Hungary's capital is small,
It is known as "Little Paris".
Streets are wide and clean,
Pavilions gorgeously appealing.
On both sides of the surging Danube,
Long embankments adorned with lush trees and flowers.
Landmark Chain Bridge spans River Danube between Buda and Pest,
From mountainsides, water rushing in a dazzling glow.
Bright moon shining on skirts and sandals,
Horses and carriages passing like flying dragons.
River embankments stretching ten miles long,
Men and women walking arm in arm.
Majestic Parliament Building and palaces,
Magnificent sights on both sides of the river.
Amusement park at night bright as broad daylight,
Illuminated with multitudes of lights immeasurable.
Sweet nomadic music of Cobza[1] floating in air,
Beautiful girls with finest skin tone whirling around.
Highly talented in music like in ancient cities

1 Referring to Hungary's musical instrument Cobza like Chinese Pipa.

Zheng and Wei[1],
The capital is also known for its warm hospitality.
Geographically a European country,
Promising as an up-and-coming star.
Imagine a hundred years from now,
Its skyscrapers will be high as sky.

布达佩斯链桥
Chain Bridge in Budapest

1 Zheng and Wei, two small countries in ancient China, both well-known for their musical merits.

荷兰
Holland 1904

瑞典
Sweden 1904

挪威
Norway 1904

英格兰
England 1904

丹麦
Denmark 1904

1904年7月19日康有为抵达英国后，次日应仙挖住公爵(1839—1916)邀请，到亨廷顿郡欣欣布鲁克豪宅小住。

6月（农历）出英伦，避暑仙挖住公爵邸舍，楼阁华严，园林之大冠英伦，盖千年诸侯旧邸，其先世随威廉入英者。此宅又为克林威尔[1]旧第，今英王尝幸之。公爵以英王卧榻浴室待予，感英故事，永夜不寐。

1 即奥利弗·克伦威尔（Oliver Cromwell，1599年4月25日—1658年9月3日），英国资产阶级革命领导人。

On July 19, 1904, Kang Youwei arrived at England. The following day, he, invited by Edward George Henry Montagu, 8th Earl of Sandwich KStJ (1839–1916), moved into his mansion for a short stay.

Traveled to England in July, I moved to the Earl of Sandwich KStJ's summer resort mansion for a short stay. The magnificence of the mansion and the huge size of its garden were unique in London. The mansion had been the former residence of noble families for hundreds of years whose ancestors came to England following King William. The mansion also had a name. Cromwell Mansion, after the English statesman Oliver Cromwell (1599–1658) and his family who once bought and lived in this mansion. It is my great honor to be invited here to stay and to be treated as a special royal guest. With a heart full of gratitude, I lie awake all night.

千年旧藩邸，百顷好林泉。
床帐金绳丽，风烟玉树圆。
通宾门置驿，爱客酒为船。
楼阁华灯靓，凭栏夜不眠。

此是克林宅，遗踪二百年。
当时起雷电，从古发民权。
游钓犹能溯，亭池自惘然。
试来摩天树，郁郁耸苍天。

今天的克林威尔豪舍
Cromwell Mansion Today

Old mansion a century of years in age,
Hundreds of acres idyllic for woods and streams.
Extravagant bedding made of gold and velvet,
Drapes embroidered with scenic trees and plants.
Served as a hotel for special guests,
Choicest wine for drinking to one's fullest.
Mansion lit shiny and bright,
Leaning against rails, I have no sleep at all night.

Once it was Cromwell Mansion,
The name was, in retrospect,
from two hundred years ago.
Unexpectedly thunder and lightening struck,
Sudden launch of civil rights movement
changed it all.
Rowing a boat and fishing meanwhile,
Pavilions and ponds in deep melancholy.
Imagine a tall magic tree flying over,
Thick green branches thrusting into the sky.

瑞典
Sweden 1904

挪威
Norway 1904

丹麦
Denmark 1904

1904 年 8 月 8 日，康有为与女儿同璧一行人从德国北部城市汉堡出发，经基尔市乘船于 8 月 9 日到达哥本哈根。8 月 12 日，丹麦首相登策尔约见康有为父女，双方交谈甚欢。由于同璧居中翻译得体自然，得到了丹麦首相高度赞叹。随后几日，康有为在哥本哈根到处参观。

On August 8, 1904, Kang Youwei and his party, including his daughter Tongbi, set off in a ship from Hamburg, a northern city in Germany, and arrived in Copenhagen on August 9. On August 12, Denmark Council President Deuntzer met Kang Youwei and his daughter, and both parties had a pleasant talk. Kang Tongbi did a good job as an interpreter and the president gave her a thumbs-up. Afterwards, Kang Youwei toured around the city for a visit.

请于丹墨国相颠沙[1]告狱吏，而观丹墨狱，庄严整洁，当为欧美之冠。看到丹麦囚犯都能住上如此豪华的场所，康有为不禁感慨万分。

丹麦韦斯特监狱 Vestre Prison（左下角图为康有为访问时原貌）
Vestre Prison, Denmark

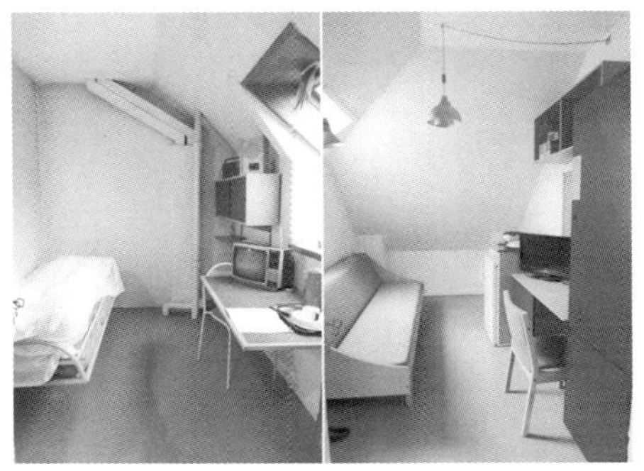

丹麦监狱博物馆（左图为 1965 年的囚室，右图为今日囚室）
Interior of a P-ison in Denmark in 1965/ Today's Prison Musuem

1 颠沙（Deuntzer），即约翰·亨利克·登策尔，1901 年 7 月 24 日—1905 年 1 月 14 日任丹麦首相。

吾游丹墨狱，华严若天堂。
壁瓦皆绿白，砖石尽红黄。
花径夹铁栏，绿草植道旁。
囚室广而洁，白铁作涸床。
食卧皆引机，橱几陈书囊。
虚空真生白，净妙倚绿墙。
倦则游憩室，草树有新芳。
时上藏书楼，或者入琴房。
妙女扬明睐，鼓琴声铿锵。
食则兼牛鱼，饮酪诚芬香。
夕赐酒半樽，薄醉可徜徉。
其厨及沐室，华整何堂皇。
费金二百万，伟哉大道场。
严丽冠各国，欧美无可方。
欧土各王宫，逊此妙丽庄。
况我富贵家，享受远相让。
回顾吾国人，室屋卑污方。
秽恶交腾蒸，疾病多疡疮。

不知卫生法，况识安乐乡。

狱囚更何论，瘐死幸有丧。

狱吏问我国，狱室可清凉。

吾颜如渥丹，忸怩无可藏。

相去何太远，天壤乃王郎。

我实政不仁，宜其国不强。

颇闻欧人风，竞侈为荣光。

争夸恤狱仁，过丽得无亢。

罚罪似赏功，差等无杪芒。

吾未敢谓然，悬此待禹汤[1]。

1 禹汤，禹和商汤，被视为贤明君主的典范。

Kang Youwei asked Denmark's Prime Minister Deuntzer to inform the prison head about his visit. The prison was stately and dignified in manner, topping all other prisons in Europe and America. The humane and comfortable living conditions of the prisoners astonished Kang to a great extent.

I came to a Denmark prison for a visit,
Astonished at its dignified look as if heaven.
Green and white its tile colors,
Yellow and red its brick colors.
Iron fences standing between flowery paths,
Roads flanked with green grass.
Prisoners' rooms big and clean,
Beds made of white iron.
Beds and tables both wall-mounted,
Bags of books kept in wall cabinets.
All rooms painted greyish-green neat and clean,
Roomy lounges for leisure time.
Lush growth of trees and grass,
With air full of fragrance pleasant.
Reading books in library,

Playing music in piano room.
Charming girls flirting with eyes bright and clear,
Piano and drums loud and vibrant.
Beef and fish on daily menu,
Cheese and cream smelling inviting.
Half a bottle of wine given for dinner,
Slightly drunk and tipsy, not a problem.
Designs of kitchen and bathroom,
Modern and comfy.
Cost of construction two million dollars,
Lavish project making unrivalled facility.
The prison, awesome and unparalleled,
Topping all countries including Europe and America.
Even palaces all over the land in Europe,
Pale by comparison with such architecture.
Let alone my well-to-do home in China,
Can't be compared in terms of life enjoyment.
Looking back at my country people,
Their living condition dirty and poor.
Filthy and foul environment,
Coupled with unhygienic way of living,
Causes of sickness either from infection or contamination.
Paying little attention to personal hygiene,
Impossible to enjoy a life happy and healthy.

Even worse were the Chinese prisoners,
Maltreatment and death in prison a frequent occurrence.
Being asked by a prison officer about prison condition in China,
I, blushed scarlet with shame, could find nowhere to hide.
The gap was too enormous,
In heaven and earth, a shame like such, unspeakable.
Inhumane policies all due to weakness of the nation.
Learned about the European culture,
Regarding extravagance as boastful honor.
Striving to be benevolent and merciful,
Competing in spending for prison decency.
Punishments for faults handled like giving rewards for good,
There weren't many differences between the two.
Being not in the position to comment,
I had to leave this matter to a wise and enlightened king someday.

1904年9月9日，康有为从瑞典斯德哥尔摩重返丹麦哥本哈根。

On September 9, 1904, Kang Youwei went back to Copenhagen, Denmark from Stockholm, Sweden.

七月杪，自瑞京还，再游丹墨公园[1]，与同璧女歌曲，怅触乡国，步纍起愁。

丹墨公园水塘曲，依稀似我澹如楼[2]。
十年久绝乡园梦，万里来为波海游。
花径同携歌旧曲，柳塘小棹泛新舟。
电灯千亿游人万，泽畔行吟独起愁。

1 丹墨公园，即哥本哈根百戏园，今称趣伏里公园。

2 澹如楼，康有为年轻时在故乡南海读书二十年的塔楼。

Back to Denmark from Sweden, Tongbi and I came to Tivoli Gardens again. While walking, we recited poems, our melancholy steps kicking off deep nostalgia.

Park in Denmark, pond water humming soft melody,
Reminds me again of my beloved Danru Pavilion.
Ten-year long life in exile cut me off from my homeland dream,
Ten thousand miles of sea waves carrying me from place to place.
Walking and singing old songs along flowery paths,
Rowing a new boat in the willow shaded pond.
Thousands of lights, ten thousands of tourists,
While I, chanting poems, sank into a deep melancholy.

丹墨公园水塘楼阁，极似吾家园澹如楼。十年去国，携同璧女游此，感怆于怀。

廿年读书处，忆我澹如楼。

飞阁临波影，圆窗照道周。

横塘堤树密，对岸画堂幽。

岂意长飘泊，离乡已十秋。

哥本哈根百戏园，今趣伏里公园

Tivoli Gardens, Copenhagen, Denmark

In the quiet corner of a park in Denmark, I came across a pavilion which had a close resemblance to Danru Pavilion[1] in my hometown Yintang. Tongbi and I toured around in the park, chanting poems while walking along the flowery paths. As always, the sweet park scenes aroused a strong sense of homesickness in our hearts.

Danru Pavilion,
a sweet building etched in my heart,
Twenty years of study in it,
a memory never fading away.
Elegant pavilion reflected in surrounding clean water,
Circular windows looking out to the roads around.
Trees growing thick on the bank,
Painting hall situated across the tranquil pond.
Never thought my wandering life could be this long,
Ten autumnal seasons have already passed.

1 Danru Pavilion in which young Kang Youwei studied for 20 years.

澹如楼 - 康园

Danru Pavilion

瑞典
Sweden 1904

挪威
Norway 1904

丹麦
Denmark 1904

1904年8月16日，康有为与女儿同璧、女婿罗昌一行人从哥本哈根前往挪威首都克里斯蒂安尼亚（今改称奥斯陆）。

On August 16, 1904, Kang Youwei, along with his daughter Tongbi, son-in-law Luo Chang, went from Copenhagen, Denmark to Norway's capital Oslo.

"挪威"，意为"通往北方之路"，是北欧五国之一
Norway, One of the Five Countries in North Europe

挪威海道，万岛飞绿，扑入船中，得鲜虾，与女同璧及罗昌文仲饮酒。睹吾免冠发半白，谓五年前无此。为之叹息，口占赠罗生。

频经国难忽华颠，南北重逢已五年。

美酒空为人送老，飞舲且作客游仙。

好山缥缈欲飞去，大海盘旋几变迁。

且喜英才能磊落，又来弱女慰缠绵。

（注：罗生年弱冠，中西学并茂，兼通东西哲理。）

Sailing along Norwegian sea passage, multitudes of islands shooting out a color of green, live shrimps jumping into the boat, drinking wine with Tongbi and Luo Chang in a small houseboat. Luo Chang found my hair turning half gray, saying it was not the same as five years ago. He regretted my fast aging, heaving sighs one after another. I improvised a poem for him:

Frequent national calamities made me age fast,
Our difficult reunion after a span of five years.
Emptying wine cups to bid me goodbye,
This houseboat carrying guests to fairyland.
Mountains hiding in mist seemingly floating away,
Ocean waters turning, witnessing changes of time.
You, a brilliant outstanding young man,
Along with my tender daughter, bringing me warm comfort.

(Luo Chang is a bright young man, gifted in Chinese and Western learning and proficient in Eastern and Western Philosophy.)

苏格兰
Scotland 1904

荷兰
Holland 1904

瑞典
Sweden 1904

挪威
Norway 1904

丹麦
Denmark 1904

“天下山水之美，瑞典第一；瑞典山水之美，以稍士巴顿为第一。”

康有为于1904年8月初抵达瑞典的斯德哥尔摩。那次旅行正值在美读书的二女康同璧暑假，偕父同行，下榻在稍士巴顿的大客舍。波罗的海南部山岛的夏日景色秀丽诱人，隔绝凡响，实为人间乐园。父女俩被深深吸引，不舍离去。两年后，康有为重赴瑞典，因喜稍士巴顿的山川之美，一个月后，以六千美金之价，买下歌舒曼[1]的一片山域，以隐居之地，名曰“避岛”。岛上有几间石基结构的木屋，康有为根据各屋的用途题名：一间曰“北海庐”，以为家焉；一间小边屋曰“遁簃”，以为书斋；另一间五尺斗室曰“坐忘龛”，用于禅坐。此外康有为还利用地形的自然特点，指定“望云台”“无碍塔”“鱼钓矶”“无垢室”等，打造了一个简朴而美好的家园。那年二夫人梁随觉携女儿同复及一名西佣随夫同行，一起居住在岛上。十余月后，生四女同环。

瑞典地处北欧，一年四季在于夏。岛上住家，均为富贵人家，夏季来岛上避暑赏景。瑞典王奥斯卡的避暑胜地

1　歌舒曼（Korsholmen），瑞典海中一小岛。

也在歌舒曼，与康有为的家舍为邻，结识为友。然而夏季一过，人去岛空，好景不再。岛上的风、雪、冰使出行极为不便。寒冬季节，湖面上冻，船只停运，造成生活用品和食物的供应等难题。严寒季节对于出生在南方的康有为不甚适应。再者，隐士生活与他的救国大志也不相配。康有为于 1908 年 7 月将那房屋售还于原业主，离开“避岛”。1909 年康有为虽再次游欧，但未回瑞典。这段历史虽为简短，瑞典人颇为纪念，将康有为曾经住过的“避岛”更名为“康有为岛”。

康有为在《避岛十三咏》里，以诗歌形式描绘出“避岛”的生态环境，是他岛上生活的真实写照。

① 北海庐 North Sea Lodge ② 遁簃 Study on the island ③ 坐忘龛 A niche for meditation ④ 光明无碍塔 Tower with clear views ⑤ 望云台 Clouds watching platform ⑥ 崎岖嶝 Rocky pedals ⑦ 翠屏嶂 Emerald cliff screen ⑧ 寥一天 Top of the cliff ⑨ 松浪崎 Sound of pine waves ⑩ 松径 Pine tree trail ⑪. 鱼钓矶 Flat Rock for fishing ⑫ 无垢室 Body cleansing pool

"Among the best sceneries in the world, Sweden is number one; Among the best sceneries in Sweden, Saltsjöbaden is number one."

In August 1904, Kang Youwei arrived in Stockholm, Sweden. Along with him was his second daughter Tongbi, who, as a student in America, was on summer vacation. They stayed at the Grand Hotel in Saltsjöbaden. Both of them were greatly impressed by the exceptional beauty of the scenery in the south of Baltic Sea. Two years later in August, Kang Youwei returned to Sweden. His deep love of the superb view of the mountains and lakes there led him to purchase a mountainous area in Korsholmen island for about $6000, to be used as his hideaway place. He named it "Hideaway Island." Several old wood/stone structured houses, that Kang Youwei named poetically, were used as a house for living, a small study and niche for meditation. Taking advantage of the natural terrain, Kang designated a few places to be his locations for watching clouds, fishing, bathing, etc. His second wife Liang Suijue, bringing with their daughter Tongfu and a maid, came to the island to be with him. Ten months later in 1907, their fourth daughter Tonghuan was born.

Sweden is located in north Europe. The best season of a year is summer. The residences on Korsholmen all belonged to wealthy families who came to the island, only in summer, to stay away from the heat and enjoy the scenery. The Swedish King Oscar's summer resort was also on Korsholmen, neighboring with Kang Youwei and so they became friends. When summer was over, the vacationers left, leaving the once idyllic and lively island empty. A winter combination of wind, snow and ice made outdoor activities difficult. The supply of food and daily necessities also became a problem when the lake was frozen in severe winter. Life and weather were hard on Kang, a southerner from Guangdong. Since living as a recluse conflicted with his devotion to make Chine better, Kang Youwei decided to leave the island. He sold the island back to its original owner in July 1908. He never went back to Sweden afterwards. Swedish people named the island, his once "Hideaway Island","Kang Youwei Island" as a remembrance of his stay.

In the following thirteen poems, Kang Youwei presented a truthful picture of his "Hideaway Island" and his life on it.

避岛十三咏

13 Poems of Hideaway Island

在瑞典京南湖

绝域湖海中，松石环齿齿。
买山知非年，避地亦几几。

South Lake of Baltic Sea in Sweden

The spectacular island in south lake of Baltic Sea,
Densely encircled by pine trees and rocks.
Buying the mountain reminds me of my fifty years of uncertain life,
Using the island to be a place for me to hide away.

北海庐

结庐依北海，更在海中岛。

高想钓璜人，遁世心乐苦。

North Sea Lodge

A lodge stands by the North Sea,
In fact it stands on the island amid the sea.
Missing my enlightened Majesty,
Living as a recluse,
a heart tangled with bitter sweetness.

遁簃

崖下安乐窝，书画可隐坐。

谁知肥遁客，穷发来高卧。

（在北海庐后十丈）

Study on the Island

Under the cliff sits a secluded side house,

To be used for reading and painting in comfort.

Who knows me, a fat foreigner?

Living on this barren island in total complacency.

(Side house is ten *zhang* behind North Sea Lodge)

坐忘龛 （也称广忠堂）

小龛五尺余，松阴作禅坐。

清磬一声闻，却忘天地大。

（在遁簃西）

A Niche for Meditation

A niche a little over five feet,
For me to meditate in the shade of pine trees.
Startled by a sudden crispy noise from a flat stone,
Reminded of the immensity of the Heaven and Earth outside.

(Located at the west of the study.)

瑞典“避岛”，1907 年冬

Picture Taken on Hideaway Island in the Winter of 1907

光明无碍塔

琉琉四面壁，帝网重重隔。
光明四无碍，尽揽湖山白。

（北海庐中西三层）

Tower with Clear Views

A tower with splendid views on all four sides,
No more hostile snare and trap around.
Bright glow unhindered on all sides,
Enabling full view of the lakes and mountains.

(Referring to the third story attic in the west wing of North Sea Lodge.)

望云台

穷发数万里，思亲上石台。

倚松望天末，东海片云来。

Clouds Watching Platform

Being exiled to this barren place from thousands of miles away,
Missing relatives, I stand on the stone platform.
Leaning against a pine tree and lifting eyes towards end of the sky,
Clouds rolling and moving from the east sea.

崎岖嶝

石磴崎岖登，缘崖草花绿。

世路更险峨，休嫌此却曲。

Rocky Pedals

Rough rocky pedals hard to climb,

Cliffs nearby cloaked in green grass and flowers.

A lot rougher is the road of life,

No complaint about this twist and turns underfoot.

翠屏嶂

屋后倚翠屏，苍苍擘崖嶂。

松盖何亭亭，明月上一丈。

Emerald Cliff Screen

Behind the house an emerald screen stretches,
Green foliage hangs full over the rock face.
Lush pine trees stand straight and tall,
Bright moon emerges ten feet taller.

寥一天

松风何寥寥，绝顶俯万壑。

长天浩无穷，望极蔚蓝幕。

（在崖顶，为东岛最高处，巨石环松，吾欲营一亭名之。）

Top of the Cliff

Breeze of pine waves humming thin and low,

Top of the cliffs looking down numerous chasms.

The sky is vast and immeasurable,

And eyes cannot reach the end of its infinite blue.

(The highest spot in the east cliffs on the island.)

松浪崎

石矶盘平曲，晏坐落花深。

下有碧浪声，上有青松阴。

Sound of Pine Waves

A large rock lies flat but patchy,

Sitting idle amid fallen flowers deep.

Below the sound of green waves murmuring,

Above the shade of green pines covering.

松径

长松二百株，郁郁涛不静。

碧水青山中，扶筇行此径。

Pine Tree Trail

A trail lined with two hundred tall pine trees,
Breezy symphony winding through thicket nonstop.
In the green water and mountains,
Walking on the trail with the aid of a cane.

鱼钓矶

堤矾泊舟处，白石濯离离。

春来万鱼子，不忍钓竿垂。

Flat Rock for Fishing

At the dyke where boats mooring,

Stones washed white and clean.

Thousands of fish fries pouring in,

No heart to cast a fishing rod in.

无垢室

湖波通于海，海水冷于冰。

日脱垢衣浴，无垢天海凝。

Body Cleansing Pool

The lake connecting with the sea,
Sea water colder than ice.
Taking off dirty clothes and bathing during the day,
From the frozen sky and sea emerging as cleansed body.

另外几首“避岛”诗

Other Poems of Hideaway Island

康有为 1907 年 3 月到纽约，庆贺五十大寿。两年前在美加州演说时结识年轻貌美的何旃理，双双坠入爱河，鱼雁传书两载后，11 月于纽约纳姬旃理。12 月携新人返回瑞典“避岛”，题诗一首。

In March 1907, Kang Youwei went to New York celebrating his 50th birthday. Two years ago when he was giving a speech in California, rallying for Baohuanghui, he met a beautiful young lady, He Zhanli, who admired him greatly and took the initiative to befriend with him. The two fell in love and their love developed quickly with the exchange of love letters. Kang Youwei married He in November of 1907. In December, they went back to Saltsjöbaden together.

自美返瑞再游，稍士巴顿湖泛舟

四山围岛绿离披，放棹明湖接渡时。

一曲清歌烟水暖，漪涛[1]低唱我题诗。

Returning to Sweden from America, in a boat in Lake of Saltsjöbaden

With mountains closing on all sides,

The island cloaked in whole green.

A boat sent out in the lake to pick us,

A pleasant song warming up the foggy water,

Yitao[2] humming while I inscribed poems.

---

1 漪涛，康有为给何旃理取的新名，意为美丽动人，柔情似细水。

2 Yitao, a beautiful name Kang gave to his new wife, meaning gentle, enchanting ripples.

冬去春来，康有为居岛上一年有余，思归无望，借酒消愁。

避岛二月湖冰渐解

昨夜风翻浪涌，今朝树舞波澌。
湖上半冰半水，岛中或雪或泥。
避地有家有室，观化无住无生。
所至修垣补屋，醉来泛棹听筝。

Winter out and spring in. Having lived on the island for over a year, Kang Youwei saw little hope in his returning to his homeland.

Lake Ice Starting to Melt in February on the Hideaway Island

Last night wind stormy, waves surging,
Today tree branches dancing, waves whispering.
It's half ice, half water in the lake,
It's snow or mud on the island.
At this hideaway place,
I have both house and family,
Yet not to be bound by a place,
Following my fate should be the way.
Here and there,
The house needs fix and repair,
Now and then, getting drunk,
I ride a boat,
Drowning my woes with wine.
Vestiges of heroes only kept in songs.

同薇女久别五年，婿麦仲华曼宣与同璧女亦别经年，吾旧有“一家骨肉三洲地”之句。今同薇偕婿曼宣来瑞，璧以暑假亦来瑞，而吾乃将鬻宅矣。夜来漪涛歌舞以佐饮酒，聊以穷欢而慰别，又将分张，不胜离合之感也，戊申四月。

绝域飘零久别离，湖山买宅绿涟漪。
画堂秉烛围炉夜，红毯清歌妙舞时。
聚散悲欢聊复尔，坏空城住更安之。
三洲数载重相见，穷夜清娱且莫辞。

Kang Youwei's elder daughter Tongwei, husband Mai Zhonghua hadn't seen sister Tongbi for a few years, matching the saying "A family divided in three continents." In the summer of 1908, Tongwei, together with her husband, went to Sweden. Tongbi would also come to Sweden as soon as her summer vacation began. Kang Youwei was delighted to see daughter Tongwei. In the evening, the family got together in the living room, singing, celebrating their rare reunion.

Wandering away to an extraordinary place,
Purchasing a house in lakes luring and mountains green.
Burning candles in the living room with everyone sitting around the stove,
Great time for happy singing and dancing.
Joy or sorrow no more a big deal,
Having weathered it all making me tougher than before.
A reunion from a span of three continents and several years,
Tonight is the night we drown ourselves in happiness.

次夜饯曼宣[1]行，兼送薇、璧。酒酣听歌，呜咽不终而散。

良会听歌又几时，绕梁激楚更含悲。

炉火余红对残日，花枝转绿照清漪。

昨宵团雪今先散，他日明湖有后思。

人去楼空将舍宅，强为欢会只伤离。

Kang Youwei was sad to part with his son-in-law Manxuan, and daughters Tongwei, Tongbi at a farewell dinner.

Unknowing when to hear this singing again,
A tone so lingering and heart so wrenching.
The dying red in stove reflecting the setting sun,
Flowery branches in fall mirrored in waves clear.
Yesterday's reunion, today's separation,
My thoughts of missing them will fill the lake clear.
No point to keep the lodge when the lodgers are gone.
Cheerful reunion flips into cheerless parting.

1 曼宣，同薇夫婿。

苏格兰
Scotland 1904

荷兰
Holland 1904

瑞典
Sweden 1904

挪威
Norway 1904

丹麦
Denmark 1904

荷兰造船诗

1904 年 9 月 17 日，康有为由比利时进入荷兰。在阿姆斯特丹，他对荷兰人的造船技术十分着迷，并作了一番研究，对其成为海权强国向往不已。

On September 17, 1904, Kang Youwei entered Amsterdam, Holland from Belgium. Being fascinated with Holland's craftsmanship in shipbuilding, which had reached a high level of perfection, Kang made a thorough investigation in the shipyard in Holland, admiring their ability to build quality ships and become a maritime power.

荷兰滨海而都，以船为生，故从班、葡之后，辟新地而取南洋最早。今星架坡、澳门一带及台湾，皆荷人开辟地。与日本交通亦荷人为先，故日人外学先有兰学焉。其力之滂薄四布，亦伟大矣，则皆船之为用也。故大彼得变服而就学焉，以强其国。方寰海之大通，无船犹鸟之无翼，鱼之无翅，人之无手足也。

我国以大陆自足，享用不穷，无意营外，不注意船学，遂令世界主人之位坐让与人。此真昔者一孔之儒之大罪也！荷博物院最富于制船缩型，不让于英、法，而古则过之，可以取鉴矣。

荷于其十六纪始创海舰，当吾明末也，创人名地捞打1。遂胜英而入其太吾士河，搴英之旗今犹存焉，荷人以为光荣。然观其一千五百九十六年所制之大船，甚蠢，炮在横舱，其后船式日益改良而加精，旧样数百悉在焉。中国不可不取而制一缩型，以考进化之理，吾可一造而跃至其极也。其剖船型甚精细，令人可一望而得其内容。其二十余年之船四层。今荷船厂在此者三，皆有缩型。其大厂在哈护忽士路，其荷之船坞型甚多，其挖泥型、搅水型附之。

——《荷兰游记》

1 地捞打（De Oranjie）。

Holland was a coastal country, whose main industry was shipbuilding. Soon after Spain and Portugal's invasion in Nanyang[1]. Holland also went and set foot there, colonizing places such as Singapore, Macao and Taiwan. Holland was the first country to start a business relationship with Japan, so Holland became a country for Japanese to choose to study abroad as well. Holland, with its craftsmanship being so far ahead of the world, became a country full of power and grandeur. The seas of the earth are so enormous that without ships it would be just like birds without wings to fly, fishes without fins to swim, men without limbs to function.

My China, being content with her vast mainland yielding abundant produce, considered overseas business and shipbuilding unnecessary. Atlas, her global master seat had been taken away by others, which was a huge unpardonable mistake according to the Confucian Way. The Maritime Museum in Amsterdam holds multitudes of ship models, fine as or even better than Britain and France.

Holland's ocean shipbuilding started as early as 16th century, a period when China's Ming Dynasty was coming to an end. The creator of ocean ship was De Oranjie[2]. Once the Dutch fleet sailed up the Thames, catching the English

---

1 Nanyang: a general name used towards the end of the Qing Dynasty for Southeast Asian countries.

2 De Oranjie (the Orange): referring to Dutch royal family.

unprepared. The Dutch people, keeping their triumphant flag to this day, and are very proud of their victory in battle and excellent craftsmanship in shipbuilding. However, the design of a Dutch warship built in 1596 looked quite stupid, as the cannon was set in the transverse compartment. Afterwards, the Dutch greatly improved the designs from about a hundred older designs. China should not just copy designs from the Dutch, but make better designs or to build even more powerful ships on her own. In the museum, all the ship profiles are very precise, showing detailed inner contents. Their twenty-year old ship had four decks. This shipyard is number three in the country and the ships built here all have ship models. The leading shipyard is in Rotterdam that builds a great variety of ships, such as dredgers, cement mixer ships, etc.

—— Holland Travel Notes

荷兰舰队攻打英国舰队获胜（1667 年 6 月）

Dutch attack on the Medway ended in Dutch's victory, June 1667

睹荷兰博物院制船型长歌（节选）

荷兰先觉逐其后，聚精制舰成殊勋。荷于其十六纪始创海舰，其后船式日益改良而加精，荷人以为光荣。

纵览荷兰剖船型，感喟彼得[1]木屋勤。
蕞尔荷兰强若此，况于中华万里云。
嗟哉谁为海王图？铁舰乃是中国魂。
何当忽见铁舰五百艘，黄龙旗荡四海春！
呜呼！安得眼前突兀五百舰，横绝天地殖我民。

Dutch's shipbuilding far ahead of the world, Aiming high and reaping great achievements. Starting to build a submarine early in 16th century, Striving for excellence, their craftsmanship leading the world, Their success, the Dutch were very proud of.

1 沙俄彼得大帝，伪装成海员来到阿姆斯特丹船厂学习造船技术。

Viewing a great variety of Dutch ship models,
Marvelling at their high shipbuilding
craftsmanship.
No wonder Peter,
the Great[1] lived in a cabin as a workman,
Keen on learning how to build ships.
Holland, a small country capable of such
advanced techniques,
Why not my great China with its vast territory.
O, who holds the sovereignty over the seas?
Shipbuilding should become China's utmost priority.
Behold! In my dreamy state of mind, five
hundred steamships sailing,
In the blue sea with yellow dragon flags fluttering!
But alas! Five hundred warships appear,
looming large before my eyes,
Dominating the sea and colonizing my people.

---

1 Peter, the Tsar of Russia, who, disguising himself as a sails man, went to Holland to learn shipbuilding.

阿姆斯特丹的国家海事博物馆

The National Maritime Museum in Amsterdam

荷兰鹿特丹造船所

Shipyard in Rotterdam, Holland

沙俄彼得大帝是康有为钦佩的帝皇。他对其微服私访在荷兰造船厂当学徒的事迹大为赞叹，故而趁机来到原址参观膜拜。

Russian Tzar Peter, an emperor admired by Kang Youwei, once came to the shipyard and stayed as a workman to learn the techniques of shipbuilding. So Kang went for a special visit of the place.

彼得大帝小木屋

Cabin of Peter the Great

彼得学船之屋。

吾于大地古今豪雄圣哲，

无论若何英绝皆以为可学，

惟俄大彼得真不可及也。

万国今故，岂闻有帝王变服作工于异国，

屈身与佣保伍者数年，

以强其国者乎？

惟一大彼得而已。

方今吾中国所乏非他，全在物质。

物质之乏固多，

当海权之世尤在舰队，救急莫若是。

吾国乃无人学之，

士大夫能屈身学之乎？

何论帝王。

嗟乎！

大彼得真古今英绝之人豪也，不可及矣。

Watching Peter's cabin in which he lived to learn shipbuilding,
No matter when, where, and whatever heroes or saints,
Such a tale like Peter's had never been heard of.
Among all the nations and up to this day,
Anyone ever hear a tale about a king working as a humble apprentice for several years in foreign country?
Russian Peter, the Great, did it,
Just for the purpose to strengthen his own country.
Today's China has been in want,
In desperate want of material civilization.
Material deficiency in all aspects,
Especially in sea power sustained by a strong navy,
To defend sovereignty of the nation.
No one in China has (hard) ever been learning shipbuilding skills,
No one has ever been willing to bend himself to be an apprentice.
Not to speak of a king, alas!
Peter, the Great, a true great man in the world,
To whom, no one can be compared.

1904年9月底10月初，结束了荷兰之行的康有为还想趁机前往沙俄学习君主制改革模式，便向清廷驻荷兰公使陆征祥请求签证。陆征祥好意提醒，沙俄政府为了结好清廷，宣称一旦康、梁入境，当即拘捕移交中国。康有为这才作罢，于是动身再次前往英国，随即带女儿乘船返回阔别五年之久的北美。

Between end of September and beginning of October 1904, Kang Youwei ended his travel in Holland. He intended to go to Russia to learn from their Monarchy Reform Model, trying to get a visa to Russia from Qing court envoy to the Netherlands Mr. Lu Zhengxiang. Mr. Lu, out of his kindness, warned Kang that he would be arrested on his arrival and handed over to Qing Court, as the Tsarist government wanted to keep a good relationship with Qing Court. Kang Youwei had to give up this plan and set off to England again. There he would unite with his daughter and return to North America by ship.

苏格兰
Scotland 1904

荷兰
Holland 1904

瑞典
Sweden 1904

挪威
Norway 1904

丹麦
England 1904

1904年10月4日，康有为从荷兰返回英国，访问苏格兰。康有为往访苏格兰爱丁堡瓦特故居，对其发明的蒸汽机之赞颂、艳羡，无以复加，以迟来而自责，所用笔墨更浓更重：

虽光电诸学有以佐成之，
非一人之功，
然瓦特未出之前一世宙，
瓦特已出之后一世宙，
具大法力，转大法轮，
有功德于世，孰有若瓦特者乎！

On October 4, 1904, Kang Youwei returned to England from Holland. Then he made a visit to Scotland. Kang Youwei visited steam engine inventor Watt's former residence in Edinburgh. Admiring and praising the steam engine, he regretted not coming sooner. He wrote a poem in a lofty admiration of the inventor Watt:

Electricity had been invented through a joint effort,
No individual should be solely credited.
However the world was a slow world before Watt's invention,
And the world became a different world after Watt's invention.
His invention was mighty powerful,
Powerful enough to make wheels turn.
An inventor with an immeasurable contribution to the world,
No one else but James Watt.

爱丁堡

Edinburgh

游苏格兰京噫颠堡，见创汽机者华忒[1]像，感颂神功，不可忘也。（节选）

汽机创自英华忒，水火相推自生力。
汽船铁轨自飞驰，缩地通天难推测。
万千制造师用之，卷翻大地摇天极。
百年之间器日新，凡十九万五千式。
力比人马三十倍，进化神速比例识。
我今周游全地球，足迹踏遍廿馀国。
文野诡奇尽见之，吾华前哲无此福。
游苏格兰见公像，惟公赐我生感激。
巧夺造化代天工，制新世界真大德。
华忒生后世光华，华忒未生世暗塞。
美哉神功在地球，永永歌颂我心恻。

1　华忒，即瓦特。

Visiting the National Museum of Scotland in Edinburgh, I saw the portrait of James Watt and the oldest steam engine he invented. His marvelous invention benefiting the whole of mankind should be always remembered.

蒸汽机发明家詹姆斯·瓦特（1736–1819）

James Watt, Steam Engine Inventor (1736–1819)

Steam engine invented by James Watt,
Its power generated through water and fire.
Driving steamboats and trains like a wind,
Able to shorten travel and reach further distances.
Thousands of manufacturers using his steam engine,
Tremendous changes and dramatic wonders taking place.
In a century, steam engines evolving for the better daily,
A great multitude of engineering designs springing up.
Thirty times more powerful than humans and horses,
The speed of progress amazingly swift.
I've been traveling all over the world,
My footsteps have covered over twenty countries.
Civilization and barbarism I've seen them all,
China's ex-philosophers couldn't have such an opportunity.
Touring in Scotland and seeing the portrait of Watt,
My admiring heart filled with gratitude.
Amazing invention fine as Nature's wonders,
A great contribution to mankind all over the world.
After Watt's life the world became light and bright,

Before Watt's life the world was gloomy and dark.
His wonderful creation remaining in the world,
Remembering him, I will sing his praise always.

最早的蒸汽机（苏格兰爱丁堡博物馆）

Oldest Steam Engine in exhibition at National Museum of Scotland in Edinburg

格拉斯哥（拉士高）

Glasgow

游河底隧道，长半英里，穿河底而为之。筑十年，费一百五十万镑，可谓非常之巨工矣。两岸有楼，以机下地穴，牛马车载数十吨者可下也，上亦同。得诗：

我游拉士高，中横格来河。
波平仍渺沵，欲渡唤奈何。
宁知凿河底，隧道通前坡。
邃长逾二里，闇闇灯不炧。
上盖横铁罩，两壁结灰沙。
坚固不污渫，行人如蚁过。
两极通地楼，深深十丈颇。
铁缳转机亭，升降在倏俄。
六马牵重车，直入载无蹉。
上天而入地，鬼神应惊诃。
河深二十尺，巨舰若丘阿。
船从河面驶，人在河底歌。

大工费千万，便民理不磨。

惟英擅长技，可法宜观摩。

A Visit to Glasgow

I came for a visit in Glasgow to see its underground tunnel, which stretched half a mile across the River Clyde. It took ten years and 1.5 million pounds to complete, a massive costly project indeed! Two red brick stone rotundas flanked the river as entrances. Motor vehicles and pedestrians were hauled down and up by hydraulic powered lifts. Horses and carts ten tons heavy had no problem using the tunnel. I wrote a poem about this tunnel:

Coming for a visit in Glasgow,
Where River Clyde runs across.
Waves calm, pedestrians a few,
No ferry service available.
An underground tunnel spanning the river,
From one side to the other.
The tunnel extending half a mile in length,
Darkness inside dispelled by numerous lights.
Iron sheet as tunnel roof,
Concrete walls on both sides.
Structurally strong and water proof,

Pedestrians passing like ants.
Two rotundas standing at each side as entrances,
Reaching a depth of ten *zhang*.
Hauled by hydraulic powered lifts,
Up and down in a speedy manner.
Heavy carts pulled by six horses able to enter
with no delay.
Ascending to heaven and descending to hell,
Gods and ghosts gasping in awe.
The river being twenty feet deep,
Giant ships harbored like hill mounds.
Ships sailing on river surface,
Men singing at river bottom.
Millions of pounds the cost of this elephant project,
The excuse, service for the citizens.
Made only possible with British technical abilities,
To be viewed and emulated by the world.

格来河 River Clyde

格来河隧道 Glasgow Harbor Tunnel

爱尔兰
Ireland 1909

摩纳哥（满的加罗）
Monaco 1907

墨西哥
Mexico 1905–1906

美国
America 1905

苏格兰
Scotland 1904

爱国短歌行

神州万里风泱泱，昆仑东南海为疆。
岳岭回环江河长，中开天府[1]万宝藏。
地兼三带寒暑藏，以花为国丝为裳。
百品杂陈饮馔良，地大物博冠万方。
我祖黄帝传百世，一姓四五垓兄弟。
族谱历史五千载，大地文明无我逮。
全国语文同一致，武功一统垂文治。
四裔[2]入贡怀威惠，用我文化服我制，
亚洲独尊主人位。
今为万国竞争时，惟我广土众民霸国资，
遍鉴百国无似之。
我人齐心发愤可突飞，速成学艺与汽机。
民兵千万选健儿，大造铁舰游天池，
舞破大地黄龙旗。

1 天府，意指四川盆地被称为天府之国，养育中华民族的粮仓。
2 四裔，这里是指朝鲜、琉球、安南、暹罗。

Song of Patriotism

Beyond ten-thousand miles in distance,
Wind blowing across the Divine Land.
From south-eastern Mount Kunlun to the sea,
Is the border of our territory.
Meandering Mountain ranges, endless river flows,
In the middle sits the basined land of abundance Tian Fu[1].
Blessed with three geographic zones and a spring-like climate,
Flowers as our kingdom and silk as our rich garments.
Bountiful produce, everlasting supply of food and drink,
Her vast territory and profuse resources,
Nowhere else can compare.
Our ancestor Yellow Emperor[2] from centuries ago,
All men are brothers within the four seas.
Our China has written five thousand years of history,
Our civilization much ahead of other countries.

---

1 Tian Fu: a self—sufficient and natural granary in Sichuan Province.

2 Yellow Emperor, a legendary ruler, who unified China and started civilization.

Mandarin is a unified language in the country,
Unification by force and ruling with enforced culture.
Four neighbouring countries[1] come to pay tribute with gratitude,
Accepting our culture and convinced of our system,
China has enjoyed a sure position of dominance in Asia.
Today the world has entered an era of competition,
Our land vast, population large, resources abundant,
No equal can be found throughout the world.
Solidarity will make our people powerful and strong,
Going all out acquiring technology and learning steam engines.
Elite troops chosen from thousands of militia,
Shipbuilding and naval construction both a priority,
Waving of yellow dragon flags vigorously over the land of China.

1 Four neighbouring countries refer to Korea, Ryukyu (Japan), Annam (Vietnam), Siam (Thailand).

罗生枝利开十八年，已成大市，地暖宜果，病者多来避居。

寒山夹大野，极绿拓平芜。

土沃耕农富，天和病客租。

丘陵成缛绣，花果足菜铺。

廿载诛茅棘，居然盛大都。

Having been developed for only eighteen years, Los Angeles has become a large city. Its warm weather all year round is good for health recuperation.

Between cold mountains stretch vast plains,
Green plantation taking gradual control of barren land.
Fertile fields enable farmers to grow rich,
Agreeable climate suitable for ailing guests.
Hillsides transformed to gorgeous embroidery,
Flowers and fruits displaying exuberance in pride.
A settlement for living of only twenty years,
A large and flourishing metropolis it's become.

纽约楼阁高二三十层，初到惊睹，冠大地矣。

铁构巍巍云表腾，纽约楼阁欲飞升。

十二层楼为阆苑，银行街上更卅层。

The skyscrapers in New York have twenty to thirty stores. I was stunned when I first saw a cluster of tall buildings that cannot be seen elsewhere.

Holding rails tight with shaky hands,
Looking out, New York's skyscrapers seem to be floating.
Buildings twelve stories high like fairyland,
Buildings go higher, to thirty stories on Wall Street.

丹壁观瀑，为园中最佳处。美人自夸甚至。危崖峭慓，日蒸无避，吾游苦之。

瀑布小以短，山崖崩以颓。
峭壁泻丹黄，危土流素灰。
草树皆不产，童髡无徘徊。
炎日照蒸酷，难觅松阴开。
俯瞰徒惴慓，徒闻转谷雷。
小坐亦无所，佳趣何有哉？
危栏空徙倚，不如归去来。

瀑布小以短，山崖崩以颓。

Waterfalls small and short, Cliffs cracking and disintegrating.

Tower Fall is a waterfall said to be the most worthy of sightseeing in the Tower Creek region in the state of Colorado. The place is actually not as good as it's been described. Touring around, I was exhausted walking on dangerous and steep cliffs under the heat of a scorching sun.

Waterfalls small and short,
Cliffs cracking and disintegrating.
Yellow muddy flows rushing down from precipices,
Crumbling soil dust permeating the air.
Barren land without a touch of green,
Few kids to be seen around.
Scorching sun hot as a furnace,
No shade to be found for a break.
Looking down from the height, my legs giving way.
Startled at sudden noises like thunder echoing in the valley.
Nowhere can be taken as a seat for a while,
No fun at all is it to stay here.
Dangerous railing unsafe to lean on,
Rather turn round and go home.

落机山尽处，行自要离[1]至思父士顿山道[2]中七十里，九月白雪满山，岩壑甚美。

At the end of Rocky Mountains, there is a road named the Million Dollar Highway—the stretch between Ouray and Silverton, both of which are old small towns in the southern part of Colorado. The snow-white mountain scenes in September are spectacular and breathtaking.

1 要离，即 Ouray，科罗拉多州乌雷县。

2 思父士顿，即 Silverton，科罗拉多州锡尔弗顿镇。

群峰连白雪，山路缘幽林。
六马曳大车，垂坂千百吟。
涧流积碧绿，青松荫渊浔。
积水转金轮，制电照崎嵚。
千室放光明，矿道炳幽深。
中午到山椒，去海二千寻。
突兀耸青天，太白[1]欲摩侵，
元气通鸿蒙，美洲横古今。
南通安底斯，新国吾所钦。
东望太平洋[2]，故国动越吟。
自兹下崇崖，马佚不可擒。
一时三十里，倏下坡陀岑。
石壁峙嶙峋，积铁立竦森。
流水自湝湝，牛群牧松阴。
时有烟剪人，板屋临绿浔。

1　太白，即金星。

2　从中国人的习惯来讲是东望太平洋，但康有为此时是在美洲，应为西望太平洋。在翻译的语句中，更正为“西望太平洋”。

亦有开矿夫，帐幕淘取金。
此地落机尽，万峰攒花心。
故擅岩壑美，铁轨新酌斟。
晚归卧汽车，溪石听佳音。

石壁峙嶙峋，积铁立竦森。
Peculiar rocky walls standing by the sides, Forest trees tidy and neat like iron building blocks.

White snow-capped mountain ranges,
Mountain roads hidden in green thicket.
Riding in a carriage pulled by six horses,
Its buckboards humming along as if singing.
Water flows in ravines drawing a tint of green,
Pine trees shading chasms and puddles in depth.
Accumulated water turning hydraulic wheels,
Electricity generated to light the mountains.
Thousands of residences lit bright at night,
Mining roadways aglow down the pit.
Reaching San Juan at noon,
Elevation two thousand meters above sea level.
Ragged peaks thrusting abruptly towards the sky,
Which heavenly generals trying to touch.
Creation of the earth originating from oblivion
in the beginning,
American continent in existence long time ago.
The Andes lay on its south side,
America a new country I do admire.
Facing the Pacific Ocean in the west,
A feeling of homesick flooding my heart.
Running down the cliffs, the downhill speed
rushing the horses,

Only taking one hour to reach Silverton.
Peculiar rocky walls standing by the sides,
Forest trees tidy and neat like iron building blocks.
Stream water gushing along elegantly,
Herds of cattle grazing on pine-shaded pastures.
Sometimes encountering Indians,
Their wooden houses covered in green by waterside.
Sometimes passing by gold miners,
Washing for gold by their tents.
Here's the end of Rocky Mountain,
Layered mountain peaks as if flower patels.
The most diverse and beautiful mountain terrains,
Attracting railways to be built here.
Returning at night and sleeping in a sleeping car,
Listening to melody formed by the streams.

遍游北美，将往南美，巴西辟新地。1905.10

平生悲悯天人志，开辟榛荒宙合图。
流落天涯谁或使，纵横瀛海气遍粗。
手扶旧国开云雾，足踏新洲遍海隅。
惯历诸天经万劫，教宗国土此区区。

Having toured around most places in North America, I will go to South America, Brazil for new exploration.

A humble and empathetic man I am,
With a keen mind, knowledge, intelligence.
Striving to open up untamed land for a new universe,
Who should be held accountable for my exile?
Being driven to cross the vast ocean,
Courageous and undaunted I was transformed
to a new me.
Hands dispersing clouds shadowing my old country,
Feet stepping on new continents,
covering seaside nooks.
Having gone through calamities time and again,
Papal land very much limited.

爱尔兰
Ireland 1909

摩纳哥（满的加罗）
Monaco 1907

墨西哥
Mexico 1905–1906

美国
America 1905

苏格兰
Scotland 1904

1905 年 10 月，正在美国南部游历的康有为，因倡导各地保皇会发动抵制美货，拒绝中美续签排华法案的运动他身处危险，急忙于 1905 年 12 月 2 日离开美国，入墨西哥躲避。他滞留在莱苑（托雷翁），撰写欧洲游记。

1906 年 1 月 26 日，康有为乘火车沿中央铁路南下入墨西哥域，适逢墨总统外出未得见。

The 1905's boycott of American goods in China led by Kang Youwei put him in danger, so he left America in a hurry on Dec. 2, 1905, seeking shelter in Mexico. He overstayed in Torreon, concentrating on writing travel accounts.

On Jan. 26, 1906, Kang Youwei took a train via south-bound Central Railway, entering Mexico. He tried to meet Mexico president, yet it didn't happen.

入墨国境

丙午正月自美国南游墨西哥，贯其南北全境。自是稍倦游矣。

历亚欧非到美洲，冬残墨国又来游。

海山踏遍廿万里，国土纵横大九洲。

政俗诡奇文野见，榛荒开辟古今遒。

诸天未历吾犹憾，老子婆娑纳地球。

Entering Mexico

In January 1906, I went southward to Mexico from the United States. Having toured around Mexico from the north to the south, I was kind of tired.

From Asia, Europe, Africa to America,
I came to Mexico as winter drew to its end.
Traversing mountains and sea two-hundred thousand *li*,
And national territories across nine continents.
Here politics weird and culture wild,
Untamed land development on a mix of ancient and modern land.
Infinity of heaven discovered through astronomical observation,
Meditating Lao Zi's teaching of unity of heaven and earth.

游墨西哥

贯其南北，母山[1]为脊，左右斜落为平原。地瘠苦，二千里不生草木。税重民贫，天寒皆无衣褐，以毡贯颈。汽车人备五色，亦诡奇之异观矣。风化杂沓，皆守旧也。

母山盘郁两洋边，徙自鲜卑[2]别有天。
地赤不毛怜石国，民贫无屦拥寒毡。
黄红白种久相杂，美法班争亦有年。
旧迹文明坛庙在，摩挲认自汉家迁。
明湖桥畔记飞鹰，走尽群山辟墨京。
人种移从丫士驾[3]，天神飞下葛爹倾[4]。
战争已久民能主，专制犹存乱岂平。
政俗少能摹美国，道涂楼阁见飞惊。

1　母山，马德雷山脉，位于墨西哥高原，由西北走向东南的山脉。
2　鲜卑，鲜卑族是广泛活动于西伯利亚一带的蒙古语族。
3　丫士驾，即阿拉斯加。
4　葛爹倾，西班牙将军葛爹（Cortes）率领士兵入侵阿芝特克首都。

Mexico-Tenochtitlan

Madre Mountain Range through north and south with both left and right sides inclined to stretch into plains. The land was barren, infertility obvious two thousand *li* in breadth. Taxes heavy, people poor, no warm clothes to wear in winter. Mexicans wrapped themselves in felt to keep out the cold. Passengers in different ethnic colors mixed in a train, a sight bizarre and creepy. Customs and culture confused and wild, all too antiquated and out of date.

Madre Mountain Range situated by the side of two oceans,
Migrated from Xianbei[1],
people living on a land outlandish.
Red soil impoverished, rocky land unyielding,
Walking barefooted,
people wrapping themselves in felt in winter.
A melting pot of yellow, red, and white races for generations,

1 Xianbei, an ancient nomadic nationality in Siberia.

As a result of years torn amid America,
France and Spain.
Stroking temples and altars,
traces of ancient civilization,
I thought they were migrated from Han[1].
By the bridge on a bright lake stands a statue of an eagle,
Mexico's capital established on the other side of the mountain.
Mistaking Cortes[2] from Spain for God-sent troops from heaven,
Migrants from Alaska, without taking actions, were easily conquered.
Having lived in a war-torn land for years,
Mexicans learned to self-sustain,
Yet autocratic ruling unable to maintain peace and order.
Politics and culture hardly copying America,
On top of the buildings covered in graffiti,
Eagle statues coming into view.

---

1 Han Dynasty of China.

2 Spanish commander Cortes led an expedition to Mexico.

注："墨人号称丫士惕（Aztecs），乃自丫拉士驾（Alaska）移来。西历一千五百二十一年，班人葛爹（Cortes）以马兵五百、炮十三来攻。墨人无马无炮，以为天神，遂被灭。争乱百年，总统专制如王者，乃少定之。然后事尚未定也。"

Note: The Mexicans, known as the Aztecs, were originally from Alaska. In 1521, the Cortes of Spain attacked Mexico with 500 horsemen and 13 cannons. The Mexicans had neither horses nor artillery. They thought the attackers were gods and were easily destroyed. In a hundred years of turmoil, all presidents in Mexico ruled the country autocratically like kings. There had been little stability. It's still quite uncertain regarding the country's future.

阿兹特克人的传说：鹰在仙人掌上吞吃蛇

The Legend of the Aztecs: An Eagle Eating a Snake Sat on a Cactus

近墨京架的[1]有墨前王故宫苑遗迹，人家数千依山居，泥砖平顶，满山皆桃花。

祆祠箫鼓闹荒村，来访蛮王石屋存。
亿万桃花夹流水，此山又见武陵源[2]。

On the mountaintop close to Mexico City, there was Chapultepec Castle[3], a palace of the former King of Mexico. Thousands of households lived on the hillside. Their houses, made of clay brick, had flat roofs. The mountains had a full blossom of peach flowers.

Drums in cathedral temple stirring up the wrecked village,
Barbarian king's stone house still intact.
Full blossoms of peach flowers going along the stream water,
Here again I saw Wulingyuan scenic area.

---

1 墨西哥城附近架的山（蝗虫山）有 Castillo de Chapultepec 上的古王朝古堡。

2 武陵源，中国一个风景秀丽的地方。

3 Castillo de Chapultepec, a historic hilltop castle once used for royalty.

查普尔特佩克城堡，古王朝古堡

Castillo de Chapultepec, a historic hilltop castle once used for royalty

1906 年 2 月至 3 月间，康有为南下胡克家州探寻玛雅遗址。康有为进入玛雅的客舍（旅馆），很吃惊地看到小院中的回廊，以及盛开的鲜花，和阶石上长满的藤蔓。自问：这不就是北京的上好四合院吗？怎么会在墨西哥看到这样的庭院和窗楹？

During February and March in 1906, Kang Youwei went south to explore Mayan Culture. Kang Youwei found, to his surprise, the housing architecture of Maya was very similar to quadrangle dwellings of Beijing, with a courtyard in the center and houses around.

蔑罅客舍制似北京院落，有感

小院回廊入眼惊，繁花藤蔓满阶生。
此是北京佳院落，如何墨国睹庭楹。
井边橘柚垂黄绿，瓦面松衫上杳冥。
细嗅海棠摊卷卧，忽思故国泪盈盈。

Similarity Between Mitla[1] Guest House and Beijing Quadrangle Dwellings

The hallway in the courtyard a pleasant view,
Catching my eyes were full-blown flowers,
And grown vines sprawling over the stone steps.
In dream I was in a decent courtyard in Beijing,
In reality I saw window lattices in Mexico's patio.
Tangelos hanging over the well in green and yellow,
Tile-shaped pine leaves spurting into the distance.
Breathing in crab-apple's aroma from the stalls,
Driven by a flood of homesickness into tears.

1 Mitla was one of many well—preserved archaeological sites in the Oaxaca Valley, where the cold, dry climate has preserved sites as old as 10,000 years.

"学以报国"是康有为励志教育的宗旨，他为墨西哥有美华人学校题词，激励同学们尽忠效国，努力开辟维新派在海外的首块根据地。

"Learning to serve the country" is the utmost aim of Kang Youwei's educational philosophy. He wrote an inscription for the Youmei Chinese School in Mexico, inspiring the students to be loyal and faithful to their home country, and strive to open the first overseas base for China's reform movement.

题墨国有美学校，光绪卅二年春 1906 年春

以祖国为念，以孔圣为志，逊志强力，时敏劬学，

勿忘本，勿媚外，辟地殖民，以拓新中国为任，

其可乎？

Inscription for Youwei School sping 1906

Always keep in heart your own motherland,
Always draw inspiration from teachings of Confucius.
Be humble in spirit, be strong in physique,
Be sharp-minded, and work hard in your studies.
Forget not where your roots are,
Admire not foreign countries.
To open up new territory and colonize a new China,
Your responsibility then can surely be fulfilled!

1907 年 6 月 10 日，康有为再次来到墨西哥，于 6 月 29 日到墨西哥城会晤墨西哥总统迪亚斯将军，两人相谈甚欢。康有为赞扬了迪亚斯执政三十多年来对稳定墨西哥国内政局做出的贡献，迪亚斯也肯定了康有为敢于改革的魄力。随后两人一同访问霍奇米尔科运河水利工程与阿兹特克遗址博物馆，在馆长和德国考古学家面前，康有为再次提到阿兹特克人和中国的渊源，大胆推测他们是在白令海峡[1]没分开前，迁徙到美洲的，并表示要用中文来记述墨西哥的历史，帮中国民众了解世界。迪亚斯听了非常激动，让大臣记录下这历史性的一刻，双方互赠礼物后才依依惜别。

墨总统迪亚斯将军
Mexican President General Díaz

1 白令海峡，后冰川期连接西伯利亚和阿拉斯加的海峡，是亚洲和北美洲的分界线和海上通道。

On June 10, 1907, Kang Youwei revisited Mexico. On June 29, he went to Mexico City to meet with Mexican President General Díaz. The two had a good talk. Kang Youwei praised Díaz's contribution to stabilizing Mexico's domestic political situation during his governance for over 30 years. Dias affirmed Kang Youwei's courage to reform. Then the two visited the Xochimilco Canal Water Conservancy Project and the Aztec Site Museum. In the presence of the curator and German archaeologists, Kang Youwei once again mentioned boldly the relationship between the Aztecs and Chinese, suggesting that the migrants to the America continent were ancient Xianbei people from China before the disappearance of Bering Land Bridge[1]. He said he would use Chinese to write the history of Mexico, in order to help Chinese people understand. Díaz was very excited when he heard this, and had this historic moment recorded in literature. The two sides exchanged gifts before saying goodbye.

1 The Bering Land Bridge, also called Beringia, connected Siberia and Alaska during the late Ice Age.

谒墨总统爹亚士于前墨主避暑行宫

1907.6.29（节选）

长杨驰道直如箭，离宫抗山林苑缅。
岩洞莎藓作宫门，卫兵持枪环似扇。
梯亭飙上入云峰，文琐华严开正殿。
绣衣佩剑直殿前，文叔幅巾出酬献。
握手殷勤语旧事，飒爽英姿犹隐现。
自言二十充卒伍，身经百死多锤炼。
二十八岁作将军，叱咤虎豹风云变。
至今七十有八龄，目光烂烂岩下电。
起自布衣为帝王，文治焕炳焜武战。
遍观大地各君相，骨相权奇曾未见。
天人眉宇照塞外，威武纷纭谁可殿？
民主乃以专制治，靖乱不使敌党煽。

墨从争乱历百年，赖君道辟民安宴。
誉我老国能变法，慰我英舰载出厄。
祝我成功天助祥，问我来游欲何得。

日命绣衣陪乘游，请我观兵阵旋抽。

将军拥旄校督卒，枪戟森森和佩璆。

陪登大学藏书楼，侁侁冑子图画大九洲。

凿渠百里泻泥湫，京邑爽垲赖此沟。

大工未竣延我筹，特乘花车出郊丘。

历言古迹请勾留，索我游记欲代译，

惜哉未成谢意周。

嗟乎！惟天下之英雄，乃相敬而相攸。

询我墨种所自由，答从鲜卑夏种留。

甘渣甲峡昔未拆，鸦拉士驾频索求。

避寒遵海渐南下，墨秘腴暖田宅悠。

中华宫坛有遗迹，沃架丹[1]宫可以搜。

总统欣命史臣记，古文大册用相酬。

呜呼！惟天下之英雄，乃相敬而相攸。

1 沃架丹（Yucatan，今译尤卡坦），墨西哥的一个州。

Meeting with Díaz, President of Mexico in Presidential Summer Palace

A straight road reaching swiftly to Presidential Summer Palace,
Located on a hill amid flourishing trees.
A cave opening covered with Salsa moss served as a gate,
Armed guards standing in circular form.
Temple stairways soaring into clouds,
Main hall opened up in majesty.
Dressed in embroidered garments, President Díaz stood upright wearing a sword,
Shrewd and sagacious, his appearance impressive.
Graceful handshaking, warm conversation about bygones,
Valiant and heroic bearing of old days still showing.
He talked about his military career starting at the age of twenty,
A veteran in battles at the risk of life.
Becoming a general at the age of twenty-eight,
Killing tigers and leopards, turning defeat into victory.

At the present age of seventy-eight,
His eyes still brimming with radiance and vigor.
Starting from a commoner to a royal king,
Ruling the country with both civil and martial virtues.
Universally true all royal appearances
handsome and good-looking,
Rarely did I come across a face scrawny and unsightly.
A celestial man with an imposing look,
Who could put him at the rear?
Autocratic ruling to maintain democracy,
And to quell rebellions instigated by foe party.
Having experienced wars and turmoil for a century,
Mexicans relying at ease on royal rule.
He praised the reform in my old country,
He heard British warship coming to my rescue.
Wishing me success with heaven's blessings,
Asking me what my purpose was to travel to Mexico.
Wearing embroidered garments and showing
me around,
Inviting me to watch the military parade.
Attended with a large retinue, the General
inspecting soldiers,
Mighty in spirit and gallant in bearing.
Walking me upstairs in the university library,
Aristocratic students busy learning all about

nine continents.
A huge construction was underway to dig a channel a hundred-mile long,
To keep the capital city nice and dry.
To avoid the blocked traffic,
We rode a flowery car to see suburbia.
The historical moment was recorded in words,
Yet without translation, my travel dairy making no sense.
Alas! Heroes of the world with mutual respect and in good harmony.

Inquiring me politely where Mexicans came from,
"Descendents from Xianbei people" was my answer.
In the age when Bering Land Bridge existed,
Survival conditions in Alaska too harsh.
Driven by freezing weather, migrants crossing Beringia,
Seeking warm weather and fertile land in Mexico.
Evidences could be traced in the palace of China,
As well as in palace of Yucatan.
President, very pleased, ordered his secretary to jot it down,
Historic record will be highly rewarding.
Alas! Heroes of the world with mutual respect and in good harmony.

爱尔兰
Ireland 1909

摩纳哥（满的加罗）
Monaco 1907

墨西哥
Mexico 1905–1906

美国
America 1905

康有为于 1907 年 1 月 25 日，从法国的奸悟[1]来到摩纳哥行政区满的加罗。他写道：“其国之特异，实为欧地所艳称，而大地所寡有。依荒山凭峻岭，绝海疆而立国，人口仅两万，如吾中国之山海间荒乡耳。然以此弹丸而立国欧土，不灭而特立，与英、德、法、俄、奥并峙而无所属，其特异一也。其特异二，欧土事情诡异，以此弹丸国而自立，实吾中国人所梦想不到。而此弹丸国之繁丽华妙，甲欧洲各大国，尤为大地人所梦想不到，亦满的加罗侯所梦想不到也……惟此区区侯国[2]，绝无苛政，遇客极厚，而昕客所为，又无警吏、报论之伺察。所以最供人欲者，不外乎声色、服食、室器数事，其日讲求以致精极妙，因以极速之率，遴甲欧土，乃自然之理，不足怪也。所可怪者，仍是海滨能存一独立侯国，不收他税，独收博税之一事耳。然其展转相成，遂成一极怪之极乐国，乃知春秋之郑、卫声色独盛，非无故也。”

1　奸悟（Cannes），即戛纳。

2　侯国，小王国。

On January 25, 1907, Kang Youwei visited Monte Carlo, an administrative area of Monaco, via Cannes, France. What he saw there surprised him greatly: a land with barren mountains on one side and the Mediterranean Sea on the other; a territory no larger than a piece of infertile land amid mountains and sea in China, yet a land with extraordinary abundances of wealth. Monaco was the second smallest independent state in the world with a population of twenty thousand people only. In history, the state was linked closely to France, yet suffered no Western imperialism from other European countries, such as England or Germany. The principality, though tiny, surpassed all other European powers with its prosperity and wealth. What had made it an international success was its extravagance and glitzy display of luxuries, which attracted flocks of tourists. The biggest draw was its simple governance and easy tax rules, enabling people to keep most of their wealth in their pockets. Influenced by mild oceanic climate, Monaco stayed lavishly green all year round. That's why an extremely small country turned into an extremely entertaining country.

大地极乐国，曰满的加罗。境土二十里，小侯何幺麽。
山海翩翩独立旗，附庸于法仍不磨。
灭得不足以为大，苟存性命乱世过。
跨山南临地中海，云石嵯峨回紫波。
气候不寒海气活，深冬木青花繁多。
侯国如弹丸，侯政不繁苛。
顺人之欲从人乐，归者如市满山阿。
博场闳丽过宫殿，公园妙美百香和。
靡颜腻理四方集，遗簪隳珥深宵多。
宝钗珠履曰诡饰，锦衣玉馔加婆娑。
鸣琴利屣繁曲剧，雕墙文瓦增嵯峨。
欧土华族数十万，束于严政无奈何。
辟此桃源异国土，纵横人欲无讥诃。
汽车一日可飞至，避寒牵袂争来过。
隳辔王孙金络马，绮纨公子玉人歌。
列国帝王居无事，微行时举金叵罗。
挥金如土掷百万，踵事增华日相摩。
服馔曲乐皆第一，甲绝欧土理则那。
小侯故垒凭海噬，官阙壮丽摩天际。

月收博税百万钱，一切无征人衔惠。

旅者如家歌乐土，妙音之天何人世。

腓尼基啡之尼士[1]，欧土权桠多产异。

从极小国生诡奇，无若满的加罗极乐之怪事。

The most delightful land on this earth, undoubtedly is Monaco, the land of Monte-Carlo. Its territory tiny, its being insignificant, its national flag flying independently over mountains and waters.

Linked to France,
Yet retaining its own national sovereign.
Having suffered from imperialists' exploitation,
Yet surviving in globally troubled times.
Situated at the base of mountains on the
Mediterranean coastline,
Purple mist winding through rocks and clouds.
Warm weather all year round,
Trees green, flowers blossoming in winter.
The principality's tiny,
Its tax rules lenient,
Supporting people's desire to seek pleasure,

1 腓尼基啡之尼士，今译尼斯，法国城市。

Hustle and bustle, every day and everywhere.
Casino more luxurious than palaces,
Exuberant aromas fill beautiful parks.
Fine faces gathering from all sides,
Joyful carnivals lasting to midnight.
Jewels and ornaments dazzling,
Gorgeous garments eye-catching.
Music pleasant to the ears,
Accompanying dancing steps in stylish shoes.
Carved walls of lofty buildings,
Bringing out steep mountain shapes.
Thousands of rich Europeans indulging in
pleasures prevented in their homeland,
Because of their governments' stringent rules.
This exotic land, on the contrary,
Allowing whoever comes to deeply enjoy.
This destination can be reached in a day via train,
Cold weather can be happily avoided in this paradise.
In a stream of golden carriages,
Playful young men and girls arriving for pleasure.
The world's kings come and stay,
Dressed in simple garments,
holding a gold wine cup.
Living luxuriously and spending money like water,
Learning strategies to develop a country quickly.

Fancy dresses, food and music are all good,
Better still is this unique governance on European soil.
Castles on the land resist the sea's corrosions,
Splendid palaces reaching high and touching the sky.
No personal taxes but a million-dollar monthly income from casinos,
Makes the country's people happy.
Tourists feel at home this land of paradise,
With heavenly music echoing on earth.
Just like Nice, a city born of Phoenicia,
A state as tiny as Monaco can give birth to the outlandish pleasures of Monte-Carlo.

十九世纪摩纳哥

Monaco in 19th Century

满的加罗赌场

Casino de Monte-Carlo

爱尔兰

Ireland 1909

摩纳哥（满的加罗）

Monaco 1907

墨西哥

Mexico 1905–1906

美国

America 1905

1909 年，康有为与前港督卜力约定前往都柏林其家小住数日，顺游爱尔兰。于5月初，自伦敦启程，前往利物浦，住在离利物浦不远的一个美丽的滨海小镇兰顿那，等候自美国前来的康同璧，同游都柏林，这也是他们先前从未去过的城市。

In 1909, Kang Youwei planned to visit Dublin and Ireland afterwards. He accepted the invitation from the former Hong Kong Governor, Sir Henry Blake, to stay for a few days in his Dublin residence. In early May that year, Kang Youwei set off from London and arrived at Liverpool. He stayed in a beautiful coastal town Llandudno, Wales, which was close to Liverpool. There he waited for his daughter Tongbi to come from the United States to visit Dublin together, a city they both had never been to.

二十二日十时，自伦敦发行，乘汽车往利物浦。吾于此道，凡三往复矣。

又别伦敦渡海行[1]，汽车烟袅作雷轰。
丘原弥绿牛羊牧，楼阁飞红市道平。
风景依然吾老矣，海波历遍月将生。
重游利物浦园囿，花径寻来眼更明。

1　渡海行，指的是爱尔兰海。

Early May of 1909, I took a train from London to Liverpool. It was my third time riding along this road.

Leaving London again to travel oversea,
In a roaring train puffing a smoky trail.
Plain green hillock pastures for the cattle and sheep.
Red-roofed houses swept past along the
smooth road.
Scenery along the way remains the same,
yet I've aged,
Watching sea waves till the moon ready to arise.
It's the second time I came to the park in Liverpool,
Eyes brightened walking on the old flowery path.

游威路士[1]，宿兰顿那[2]，碧海青山，风景冠英国。

俯临碧海浪陂陀，山路回环兰顿那。

绝好峰原皆碧绿，英伦胜地此无多。

1 威路士，即英国威尔士地区（Wales）。

2 兰顿那，即英国威尔士临海城镇兰迪德诺（Llandudno）。

I traveled to Wales and stayed in Ilandudno, where the blue sea and green moutains were the best in Britain.

Overlooking the sea water embellished with charming waves,
Mountain road circling Llandudno in the background.
Magnificent landscape all beginning with a lush green touch,
A mere few are equal to a scenic beauty like this in Britain.

山路回环兰顿那
Llandudno, Wales

游威路士之卡理维垒，威路士民居，今犹窟地为宅，列于山河。

长桥横锁亘山河，故垒森森草漫陂。

百战已忘游猎盛，遗民窟宅尚岩阿。

Visited Conwy Castle and the local people living in Wales, whose dwellings are still caves in a mountain.

Along bridge stretching across River Conwy,

Amid green grassland stand age-old castles.

Wartime memories faded away,

hunting a popular game today,

Local people still dwelling in mountain caves.

卡理维垒（康维城堡）：北威尔士康维的一座防御工事，建于1283—1287

Conwy Castle is a fortification in Conwy, North Wales, built in 1283—1287

1909 年 6 月 11 日，（康同壁记述）赴英与父晤面，乃在滨海地方居住。然后同赴爱尔兰游玩月余，7 月 16 日乃附轮返南洋。

On June 11, 1909, Kang Tongbi went to meet her father in Great Britain. They stayed at a seaside city. Then they went to Ireland and stayed there for a month or so. On July 16, they traveled on sea back to Southeast Asia.

阿尔兰都会名德逋邻，其城垒、山河、公园皆以德逋邻为名。园甚大，垒甚古，山甚秀绿，吾爱其倾士汤路大园林，卅里相望，楼阁多新式，走马乐甚。

山河苑垒德逋邻，雄秀应为自立民。

走马王城临海路，园林卅里画楼新。

Ireland's capital Dublin, its castles, rivers and parks all take Dublin as a name. Dublin's parks are huge, castles age-old and mountains lovely green. We fall in love with the park on Kingston Avenue, which is huge with two ends thirty miles apart, whose beautiful temples and pavilions are diversified in designs. It is fun riding an open horse carriage to enjoy the views.

Mountain and rivers,
castles and parks all gems of Dublin,
To which Dublin's citizens should be entitled.
Sitting in the horse carriage along the seaside road inside the park,
Passing pavilions one after another,
All fresh and pleasant to eyes.

康有为七十寿辰朝服